HOOK: THE BOOSTED MAN

Hook:
The Boosted Man

Tully Zetford

NEW ENGLISH LIBRARY
TIMES MIRROR

Chapter One

Ryder Hook jumped the last three treads of the mobile pedway from space shuttle to concrete. He was onplanet again, he owned dunnage filled with costly clothes and the trivia of the wealthy, his money-belt bulged with metal, a Delling snugged to his right wrist, and he meant to enjoy himself or know the reason why.

A shocked incoherent screaming ripped apart the warm afternoon air of Mergone. Over the heads of the passengers in front of him, all abruptly stopped in their tracks, Hook saw a boil of men and women and aliens erupt from the customs house door. The passengers shrieked and began a frightening struggle to regain the pedway and the shuttle.

Hook stared past them at the violent fear-crazed mob dashing madly across the concrete towards the shuttle. These people had been made hideous. Fungoid growths dripped from their faces and naked bodies where they had ripped the clothing away in agony. They oozed. They kept up a shrill ululating screaming. Hook saw a man with one eye dangling on a long bloody-white thread and as the man ran so the other eye oozed from its socket to swing and sway about his knees. The man fell and was instantly trampled down.

'Let me past!' screamed a whey-faced Jahnian beside Hook. He lashed out, staggering a Krifman who obstructed him. 'They're diseased! They'll infect us all!'

The Krifman, a large blocky individual, recovered with the vital alacrity usual to his race. His gun appeared instantly from his sleeve, triggered by neural and electronic circuits, fired into the air as other panicking passengers crowded and collided. Hook stepped aside. Frenzy possessed these people. A moment ago they had been cheerfully heading for the customs house and a look at this world of Mergone; now they were fighting like wild animals to get back to the shuttle which had brought them from HGL starship *Talcahhuano* in orbit above.

Someone from the customs shed was shooting at the struggling passengers. A blast scythed through them. Hook saw that lethal energy strike the stewardess, standing horrified in the shuttle's airlock valve doorway. She had been a pleasant and efficient stewardess, and although built almost exactly like an Earth girl she had not been terrestrial. Her beauty had been perfectly capable of moving any man of Earth with blood in his veins. Ryder Hook hated to see that kind of waste.

'Out of my way!'

'Let me through!'

In a weltering confusion the passengers went stumbling back up the pedway, jumping and stumbling, falling and crawling, fleeing back into the shuttle. The lazy afternoon broke apart in flame and horror.

These diseased inhabitants of the planet fought amongst themselves. Mergone was only lightly populated, so Hook understood, and he guessed the disease had not spared anyone around the curve of the world. No one who stayed down here would survive. Everyone battled for a place in the shuttle.

Again the gunman blasted from the customs shed, and this time the energy whiffed away a stumbling maddened crowd of the diseased inhabitants.

Once the people of Mergone got their diseased hands on the shuttle they'd lift off, take HGL starship *Talcahuano*, and no doubt in escaping the source of the pandemic on their own planet spread it across this sector of the galaxy. Each one would be motivated only by the desire to escape.

There seemed to be a taint on the air – only seemed to be, for Hook could smell the sweet afternoon air and only surmise what dread spores it contained.

The gunman fired again and then Hook saw him. Before there was need to draw and fire, the man staggered shrieking into the open. Although of humanoid shape he was not a terrestrial. He had two eyes, however, and these dribbled away from their sockets to dangle on pulsing threads. The man fell.

Hook reached the foot of the pedway. He started up, giving the fat rump of a hysterical woman from Storton's planet a push that drove her up and through the clamouring knot of people at the airlock. Hook drove on through.

'Hurry! Hurry!' The shuttle pilot stood at the side of the airlock valve, gesticulating, horrified, shaking, and his gun still in its holster.

He was a youngster from Haeyfuong, one of the Emerald Eye

6

cluster where living conditions were as good as most places in the galaxy and better than in this sector. Hook saw without compassion and without hatred that the boy had no real conception of what to do. His concern for his passengers was commendable. Beyond that, Ryder Hook would not commit himself.

A gel-mix blob struck the handrail and passengers ducked wildly. One or two nearest the concrete were struck and those not wearing plate-fabric clothes slimed to a jelly, collapsing and deliquescing. Hook had had enough. He went up the rest of the pedway five at a time, shoving people in front of him, herding them, grabbing them by the scruffs of their necks and hauling them up, booting them on. He halted on the sill of the airlock.

'It's horrible!' said the pilot.

'Sure. Get inside and take this shuttle up, son, fast.'

'But there are –'

'I know. They're dead already. *Move!*'

Over the concrete, leaping and squirming on to the pedway, the diseased monstrosities fought and clambered. Their screaming affronted the ears. They were disintegrating even as Hook watched, as though some super-lethal mix of dis-gel had been sprayed over them with a time-hold. They presented a picture that filled the young pilot's mind with loathing.

Hook grabbed him and chucked him inside the shuttle.

He sprang in after and, turning on the thresh-hold, drew and fired a cleansing blast from the Tonota Eighty. Scrabbling hands fell away, grotesquely twisted bodies stumbled back, and for a moment the pedway lay clear.

'Up, you womb-regurgitant!' Hook yelled at the pilot.

The pilot was being sick all over the tastefully gold-carpeted metalloy deck. Passengers inside the shuttle were reacting in a variety of ways, not one of which surprised Hook. The lights gleamed on ricked mouths, and staring eyes, and gesticulating hands. The interior of the shuttle erupted in a babble of voices.

Hook valved the airlock shut. More of the grotesque monstrosities of this doomed world of Mergone surged from the customs house, and dis-gel splattered the pedway. A blast glanced from the closing airlock valve. If anyone out there shot off a Tonota Eighty, or a Martian Mega, they could blow in a shuttle hull if they kept at it long enough. Time to lift jets.

There was no longer a stewardess to calm the passengers.

Hook thrust his way through. He shook the pilot savagely;

but that young man had reached the end of his resources. Hook dumped him and ran for the controls. This shuttle was just like a million others to be found taking passengers to and from the huge, lacy, luxurious starships in orbit around the planets of the galaxy. Hook clamped in, checked the board, found everything in the green and functioning IQ, and programmed the pre-flight pattern. Moments later he was able to punch in take-off commands and the shuttle boosted from the infected earth of Mergone.

Hook hoped a few more poor doomed devils had been whiffed into a merciful nothingness by the take-off blast.

He yanked the pilot up to the control section. The boy's young face stared up at Hook, grey-green like month-old cheese forgotten alongside a refrigerator. 'Sadie,' he whispered through lips bleeding where he had bitten down to stop the screaming. 'Did you see Sadie – she was – '

'Yes,' said Ryder Hook. 'She was a nice girl. If you don't want to join her get this crate back to *Talcahhuano*.'

'Yes.' He pulled himself into the pilot's throne. 'You – '

'I'm Ryder Hook, son. If you can't do the job, I can.'

'I'm – I'm Lieutenant O'Steele. I can do it.'

O'Steele was as good as his word. That didn't surprise Hook too much. Most starship lines employed young men – either terrestrials or some other renowned space-faring race – as deck officers and they picked well. O'Steele had only reacted as he had out of the suddenness of it all, the shock and horror, and the tragedy of seeing the beautifully-shaped stewardess, Sadie, whiffed into nothingness before his eyes. Hook neither condemned nor condoned.

The boy would find another cuddly armful in time.

The shuttle speared up out of Mergone's atmosphere. O'Steele fed his calculations nicely and the on-board computer coughed out neatly precise answers. The shuttle did not have to chase the starship too far around the curve of the world. O'Steele thumbed open the screen.

'Shuttle calling *Talcahhuano*,' he said, and his voice held reasonably steadily.

The screen came on with the face of the duty officer. He was a Krifman, tough, demanding, unyielding. He was a commander. He eyed young O'Steele in the most unfriendly fashion.

'You're reporting back suspiciously early, lieutenant! How can you have completed docking down there – ?'

'I didn't! Disease – horrible – fungus – Sadie's been killed!

They're all dead down there!'

'You great nit-stupid curd!' roared Hook, and his left hand smashed the boy out of the throne as his right closed the circuit. The face of the Krifman died on the screen.

'What?' O'Steele stared up from the deck. He looked shattered, helpless.

Hook mastered himself.

'Maybe I'm wrong, O'Steele. Just hope I am! Open up the channel again and simply report you're unable to make planetfall. Don't give any more reasons.'

'I don't see – ' began O'Steele in a surly manner.

Hook put his head down and thrust his face, ugly with rage, at O'Steele.

'What you see and what you don't see matter nothing! Just do it!'

'I'm the officer in command – '

Hook lifted O'Steele by the fancy gold-laced collar and shook him. 'Do it!'

O'Steele called out again and when the Krifman commander came on the screen reported his inability to dock. Another face pushed in on the screen. Captain Copatec, commanding HGL starship *Talcahhuano*, glared out with the intemperate high-colour of a man who liked his drop between watches – and during them – and who now, as a captain and therefore not standing watch, could make the drops coalesce into a steady stream.

'What's all this about, then, lieutenant?'

O'Steele glanced at Hook, swallowed, said: 'I couldn't make planetfall, sir. There were – peculiar – circumstances against it. We'll have to return aboard ship, sir.'

Copatec's high colour betrayed a condition that would kill him inside twenty years – a brief span of life in this man's galaxy – unless he tapered off. The Krifman commander spoke quietly in the captain's ear.

Copatec bristled.

'Disease? We've had reports that three systems had been infected. If the damn stuff's arrived here – '

Hook cursed, then. There had been rumours of disease which spread in pandemic fashion to destroy the populations of those planets unlucky enough to become infected. In this solar system of Tannenbar there were fourteen planets; but only this planet they orbited, Mergone, was fully-suited for human habitation. The next planet out, Merfalla, might support life according to

9

the interstellar almanac; but it was uninhabited. The other planets were, like their counterparts elsewhere, either frozen balls of gas or liquid-mud sun-baths.

Captain Copatec had made up his mind. He did not like the decision; but it was his responsibility.

'I've three thousand people aboard my ship, lieutenant. I can't risk jeopardising their lives for your sakes, however harsh that may be. I'm sorry. I cannot take you aboard. It is more than likely that disease spores entered the shuttle.'

'But you can't!' shouted O'Steele. The enormity of the sentence hit him. 'You can't maroon us! It's death onplanet!'

'I'm sorry, O'Steele. You are an officer of HGL spacelines. You understand the meaning of duty and loyalty to your econorg.'

'But this isn't loyalty! This is murder!'

'Come now, my boy! It would be murder if I let you and your diseased passengers aboard here. Surely you see that?'

However much O'Steele argued and pleaded, Hook knew he would never alter the captain's decision. However inhumane that decision might appear, Hook knew – only too well – that in the context of the merciless whirlpool of stars, that was the only course Captain Copatec could take and remain faithful to his sworn oath as a starship commander.

Some of the passengers in the shuttle who had recovered most of their equanimity after the horrors of their ordeal below, had pushed forward to the screen separating off the control section from the passenger compartments. They had heard enough of the conversation between starship and shuttle to understand. A crowd tried to push into the control section, shouting, yelling, their fears now a million-times greater. Above the hub-bub Lieutenant O'Steele continued to plead with his captain.

'It is no use, lieutenant. We'll report this in and there will be medical teams and assistance reaching Mergone very soon.'

'But not before we're all dead in here!'

'There's nothing more I can do.'

The screen went dead.

The interior of the shuttle turned into a bedlam of shrieks and screams. Everyone knew they had been abandoned to the sweet mercies of space.

Hook shoved the pilot unceremoniously out of the throne.

'Nothing of the disease did get in, you chancrous gonil! But like a babbling fool you have condemned us to death in this goddamned shuttle!'

Chapter Two

If in these moments when the spectre of death appeared hovering over them with the inevitability of fate Ryder Hook was the most violently angry man in the whole galaxy – well, hadn't he the right to be? Wastn't all this stupid mess everyone's fault except his own? Well, then – and what was so different about that? All his life he'd been fighting back from other people's mistakes, other people's animosity, other people's intrigues. He was no paranoiac. He was no superman. But he was confoundedly angry, all the same.

And, being Ryder Hook, he could keep that rage under absolute control. He could present a cold hard front to the galaxy that no amount of taunting or inflammatory goading could break.

'We must land on planet again, immediately!' the Krifman was shouting. Like almost all his race he was hard, tough, tinged with the egomaniac's complete conviction of superiority, and yet – as Hook knew – possessing a considerable degree of the admirable qualities he claimed. Now he hauled the pilot up and glared at Hook.

'I don't know who you are, gonil! But take care of the pilot! He's the one to take us back.'

'If you return you'll be eaten away by the disease – ' began Hook with a mild tone of voice that was chopped through by the Krifman's bellow.

'Not necessarily! There must be areas on Mergone where the disease has not yet reached. We'll be safe there until the medical teams arrive.'

Hook shook his head.

'Well, I say so! We're making planetfall again. Somewhere else this time. Up in the polar regions. Safer.'

Ryder Hook had been thinking that this situation was not one in which a man could shoot, kick, punch or fight his way to safety. He would use those methods when he had to. He would as lief hit a man over the head if that would save his own life, as not. He would prefer to think his way out of a problem, and by cunning and skill reach safety. In this case that had seemed the only way out.

You can't slug the galaxy behind the ear.

But now this loud-mouthed Krifman was trying to tell him what to do.

People could and did tell Ryder Hook what to do. Usually, though, they had to speak holding a weapon in their hands, or backed by immense forces.

The babble in the passenger compartment did not so much still as polarise around these two up front, the bulky Krifman in his plate-fab clothing and his thick, rugged, hectoring face and voice, and Ryder Hook in his plain dark-grey tunic and trousers and his battered old face that looked uglier still by reason of the facial-gel disguise he still wore.

'Let's go down!'

'No! We dare not!'

The arguments raged but Hook ignored them. He pushed O'Steele out of the compartment and when the Krifman went to prevent that, Hook looked directly at the alien. He glared. He spoke quietly; but the obsessive and strange glare of madness in his face sobered the Krifman.

'We are shuttling to Mcrfalla. The almanac says it can support life. It will be rough – maybe it will be too tough for you, friend.'

The Krifman bristled.

'We Krifmans have no peers in the galaxy! No miserable Earthman can – '

'Yes, well, you can save that. If you want to let down on to Mergone again, you'll have to shoot me – and I fancy my Delling will hit you before your fancy little dis-gel job will clear your wrist-bones.' Hook broke a cardinal rule. 'If you want to try it – go on!'

The Krifman's tenseness concealed immense courage, immense powers, immense capabilities.

If he triggered the neural and electronic circuits and his little gun flicked into firing position from his sleeve – Hook would have to beat him.

The Krifman glowered at Hook, licked his lips, and said: 'There is too much risk. We would kill innocent passengers. But – one day, gonil – '

Hook sat down in the pilot's throne.

Had the positions been reversed he knew he would have had no hesitation in triggering and shooting. Innocent bystanders might have been hit; they might not have been. That would have been a chance Hook would have taken when his own life was at stake.

'These shuttles are built for a purpose. We'll have to hope this one lasts. Now get back and tell everyone to shut up and sit quietly. Conserve oxygen. It won't take too long; but you, Krifman, are in charge of keeping the innocent bystanders off my neck.'

When a starship dropped down out of ftl to orbit a planet within a solar system she would usually distribute her passengers and freight to their destinations by shuttle. A shuttle could therefore reach a considerable distance of purely interplanetary space – as distinct from interstellar like the life shells – and this craft ought to have no difficulty at all in slipping orbits out from Mergone to Merfalla. Her construction was standard. She had been powered by HGL manufactured Kriftech IP engines which could hurl her across space in vectors that could be calculated out without reference to orbits around the central star. Not quite in straight lines – for even in the hundred and first century astronomical laws still governed the passage of bodies through space – but near enough to a straight line from Mergone to Merfalla this shuttle could be driven at relatively low velocities of sub-light speeds.

The journey would not take too long. Hook shouted for O'Steele. 'Check on our air supply, son. You may know what your damned captain ordered; I don't. I want a thorough run-down in all departments. Jump!'

'But – '

Hook stretched out a black-booted foot and kicked him.

'Jump!'

Lieutenant O'Steele jumped.

When he reported back Hook did the simple calculation in his head and swore luridly about the progenitors, life-style and eating- and rutting-habits of Captain Copatec.

'The skint-living gonil! Too penny-pinching to stick a little extra reserve aboard! We'll reach Merfalla at the highest speed and turn-around these godforsaken Kriftech IP's can reach in about eight hours terran.'

'We have air for seven – '

'Then we make it stretch!'

The Krifman, whose name he had told them with a natural

13

pride they had found ludicrous in the circumstances, was Rafflans, shouldered up, angry and suspicious. 'I'm no astronaut. Explain what you mean, pakash.'

Hook let the insult by.

'The shuttle can make about .02 C. Right? It's approximately a hundred million miles – Earth miles – to Merfalla on the course we have to run. That will take us eight or eight and a half hours, given the .02 C is average speed, including acceleration, turn-over and deceleration. You work it out, clunkhead.'

'I'm going to strip your arms and legs off you, Hook, as soon as – '

'Shut your ugly face, Rafflans, and go and quieten that woman having hysterics back there. She's using up more than her fair share of oxygen. Knock her out if you have to. But keep her quiet!'

Rafflans glared; but Hook glared back, and the Krifman took himself off.

'Right, O'Steele. The course is punched in, we're going, and if the damned engines blow up, then goodbye galaxy. You just keep her nice and trim and on course.'

Hook climbed out of the throne.

'What are you going to do?'

Hook turned on the pilot.

'What I'm going to do is no concern of yours, sonny. You keep this bucket headed for Merfalla and pray to your heathen fouled-up gods that she gets there in one piece.'

O'Steele shrank into the pilot's throne. Hook had no love for browbeating youngsters; but the lieutenant had broken once and might do so again, and he was needed to make sure the shuttle wasted not a second or a mile on course.

Hook ducked his head into the passenger compartment.

Rafflans was bending over an alien woman – she was something like an Iggutarian but with a heavier jaw and brow line and no tail – and the other passengers were sitting or lying down, some talking together, others praying, and a group of five in the aisle were calmly playing cards – the thin plastic circles whipped across with deceptive flickering speed and Hook chuckled. A shark was at work there. But at least he had a hard core of rascals to call on if necessary.

He went back to the astrogation compartment. The radio was standard HGL shuttle equipment and was interplanetary in scope. This was quite normal. The trick would be to see if there were enough spares of the right kind carried to transform

14

the set into one capable of interstellar communication.

Hook loved to trick people.

Even as he worked on the rig, breaking open the spares locker, foraging for tools, letting all his electronic know-how channel skill and expertise from his brain into his fingers, transforming the circuitry, he could think with a chuckle that he would like to trick whatever local apparat net existed here. As a rule he would never cut into a net unless the emergency was foully dire. This emergency was dire; but so far he could cope.

Adapting the spares, twisting up circuits, laying out a five-dimensional path breadboard, he worked with a sureness of purpose habitual to him. Many electronics and radio men could have done what he was doing – it was not particularly clever given an accepted standard of competence – but then, who of those many radiomen could do a quarter of the other things that Hook could do? Ryder Hook was a jack of all trades in the galaxy; but anyone who assumed he was a master of none would make a mistake – a suicidal mistake.

Somewhere on a nearby world in space, certainly within ten parsecs or so, an apparat control would be functioning, dedicated to one or another econorg or system government. With those cunning organic and undetectable implants in his brain Hook could reach out and patch himself into the apparat net. Those sophisticated implants had been given him by Earth's armed services – he could sometimes bring himself to refer to them as EAS, with the corollary that as he had been a member of Intelligence they had always been called EASI, though the missions had never been that – and if for nothing else Hook would be grateful he had been recruited. Those days lay in the past. He had been Jack Kinch, the most notorious assassin of the galaxy, then; now he was Ryder Hook, his own real honest name, and a mere galactic adventurer, a loner in a galaxy of multi-system conglomerates. Hook preferred it that way.

He finished the last connection and sat back. The rig was enormous. It would have to be, given the crazy way he'd patched it up. It was almost as big as the palm of his hand – a radio set just to reach out five light years across interstellar space – as big as the palm of his hand! Clumsy and bulky it might be; it would work. Ryder Hook had made it, and Ryder Hook did not believe in making things that did not work.

He had boarded HGL starship *Talcahhuano* from that fertile and frisky little planet the inhabitants called Pantacles but

15

which most other folk called The Spaceman's Pit. You could have a good time there, and Hook had done so. But a Boosted Man had chanced to land there, and after the resultant flurry had died down, it seemed the right time to move on. His lips drew back as he considered that he had intended to have a whale of a time on Mergone. Now disease had fouled up his purpose.

Well, Pantacles was within easy reach of this crazy set he had built.

He called out and immediately within the context of the ftl communications network dialled himself through by voice to HGL central.

'Which service do you require, taynor?'

'Communications.'

Instantly: 'HGL Communications, taynor.

'I wish to place a person to person call to Taynor Shaeel.'

Mind you, that was a laugh.

His Hermaphrodite friend Shaeel had tried, often enough, to have veself called by the title ves fellow citizens of Pertan Major preferred; but nobody in the galaxy could get accustomed to using a neuter, rather than a masculine or a feminine gender. Had Hook placed the person to person call with Tayniss Shaeel he would have been as accurate.

'Taynor Shaeel has left the Imperial Centre hotel.'

'Well,' said Ryder Hook. 'For the sake of Dear Old Dirty Berti Bashti! Where's he gone?'

'Lancing, taynor. The exact forwarding address – '

Shattering through Hook's concentration on the set a series of thumps, bangs and shrieks erupted from the passenger compartment of the shuttle. Hook cursed.

'Forward a message to Taynor Shaeel. Tell him Ryder Hook is down on Merfalla and to get there with horse, foot and guns. Check?'

'Message acknowledge, taynor.'

Hook cut the connection – one of the leads was smouldering through, anyway – and burst back into the passenger compartment.

Rafflans, the Krifman, lay on the deck. The whey-faced Jahnian Rafflans had tangled with on the pedway when the doomed and diseased people had tried to board the shuttle stood now above the Krifman. In his hand the power gun bulked with chill and menacing ugliness. It was aimed at Rafflans' midriff.

'You cursed high and might Krifmans!' The Jahnian raved

in a paroxysm of fury. 'You think you're a gift to the galaxy! Well, you'll feel differently when I blow you apart!'

The Jahnian's finger whitened on the trigger.

If he pulled that trigger all the way, if he blasted the Krifman through, the blast of power would smash on to punch cleanly through the hull of the shuttle. It would blast a hole through which all the air would rush. Long before anyone could leap for a puncture-pad, the air would be gone and they'd be breathing space.

Chapter Three

In the aisle seat directly abaft the control compartment a young girl sat with a fixed and shining expression on her face. She wore a bright and cheerful yellow shirt and purple trousers with a glitter-scarf draped across her shoulders. Her hair gleamed a rich and brilliant purple beneath the lights.

Hook bent and lifted her leg. He moved with a smooth fluidity of grace that had no time for checks or interruptions. He took off her shoe. The thing was a crystal artefact with plastileather straps and emerald studs, very fashionable. He threw the shoe at the Jahnian's hand and instantly followed his projectile.

The shoe struck the gun-holding hand. The Jahnian yelped. He looked up – and Hook hit him. His left hand closed around the Jahnian's wrist. His right chopped down on the being's neck. Jahnians have doubled-collar-bones and Hook's blow broke both as well as knocking the fellow unconscious. The gun was held in a such a grip that it could not fire. Hook would have as lief broken the hand off before he would allow that constricting finger to tighten more on the trigger.

'Womb-regurgitant idiots!' Hook said. 'How the hell did he get hold of a power-gun?'

Rafflans looked sick. The Krifman elbowed himself up. He glared at Hook. 'Got it from his baggage, the gonil.'

Neither Krifman nor Earthman mentioned that one's life had been saved by the other, neither mentioned the omission. All their lives had been saved.

'They used to lock all power guns up in a starship's safe, one time,' said Hook. 'Dangerous things to have swanning about in space.'

'Yes,' said Rafflans. He stood up. He was back to his usual bulldozer form, now and started in on bellowing the passengers into sitting down. Had Hook been a routine space officer he would have wanted to hear the full story from

Rafflans; as it was he had no time for recriminatory nonsense of that sort. They were all still alive – that was what counted in this man's galaxy.

He went back to the control compartment and the girl with purple hair stopped him. She smiled.

Hook rather cared for that smile.

'My shoe, Taynor Hook, please.'

However much Ryder Hook might care for a pretty girl's smile it still wouldn't make him perform uncharacteristic actions.

'You'll have to find it yourself, tayniss.'

'My! You are a big rough bear!'

Hook abruptly lost all interest in her. Empty-headed nitwit.

About to turn away he saw the girl for whom he had reserved a particularly warm investigation at a more opportune date walk down the aisle carrying the crystal shoe. She did not smile. She handed the shoe to the purple-headed girl.

'Here you are, Myza. Stop clowning about and let Taynor Hook get on with the job.' Then, with a straight look from her grey eyes at Hook, she added: 'Thank you. You saved all our lives again.'

Hook might, under other circumstances, have found this frank and sincere approach not to his liking. But he fancied this girl was just what she looked to be. She was not pretending.

He said: 'I think that Jahnian will need some attention. Would you care to, Tayniss –'

She responded formally. 'Tayniss Elterich. Yes, I'll see to him.'

Hook fancied that if, as he expected, they dropped the formality of the taynor and tayniss, he would be as correct in addressing her, instead of miss, as fraulein. He let his harsh features crack into a kind of smile. The facial-gel didn't help that, either, and he was lop-sidedly aware he must be grimacing like a loon.

The girl Myza flounced around on the seat putting her shoe back on. Hook watched for a moment as Fraulein Elterich walked back up the aisle. She wore a simple light-blue tunic and pants, and the sight was more interesting than anything else to hand. Hook went back to the control section as Myza called after him: 'Fat chance you'll have, big bear.'

Decidedly, considered Ryder Hook, Myza was a girl to steer clear of.

Lieutenant O'Steele held the shuttle on course. Hook went

back and checked the air. His face bore a look that would have frozen the marrow in the bones of Myza had she seen it.

'Seven goddam hours, and we have to fly eight,' he said. He was a man not given to extravagant gestures. So he did not strike his fist on to the console, or put a hand to his brow; but had he done so the gesture could not more perfectly have registered his feelings.

He looked at the energy gun he had twisted from the paralysed fingers of the Jahnian. It was a Krifarm model K-twelve. Some people claimed that power gun was as good as a Tonota Eighty. Either way, they'd both make a mess of their targets. He stuffed it down into a thigh pocket. His own Tonota Eighty remained in its low-slung holster.

Whilst it would be nice to inhabit a galaxy where weapons need not be carried, as he did not live in such a place, the opportunity did not arise. Many billions of good honest citizens walked about every day and never carried or touched a gun all their lives; but they were protected by their own multi-system conglomerates and lived peacefully on a fully-settled world. Out in the galaxy between spheres of interest conditions were somewhat different.

Hook checked the air again. He made up his mind and smashed the plastic plate, reached in and juggled the control valves. He squeezed the flow. Recycling could take place on its usual scale; but without an atmosphere plant aboard all the oxygen would eventually be burned up by their bodies.

'At that,' he said, with a bleakness habitual to him. 'It should quieten 'em down back there.'

He reached down the small, orange-painted emergency oxy bottle and went forward to stand abaft the pilot's throne. He moved quietly. O'Steele just did not hear him, scant centimetres away. Hook bent and stowed the orange oxy bottle under the throne.

When he straightened up again he said: 'You're doing all right, lad. But keep awake. The air's been throttled.'

His sudden voice made O'Steele jump.

'I didn't hear – throttled? Will it last?'

'If it doesn't, son, you'll be as dead as the rest of us.'

Rafflans appeared past the screen.

The Krifman had regained his usual composure after his undignified and frightening experience.

'They're complaining they're hungry back there, Taynor Hook.'

'So am I. They'll eat when we reach Merfalla.

As a craft programmed merely to take the passengers from starship to planet no rations had been put aboard her. Some of the people found the odd biscuit, bar of chocolate, stick of latik or apple. If there was to be a share out – 'See to it, Rafflans. I want no undue exertion from here on.' He glowered at the Krifman. 'If any of 'em start playing it funny, tap them on the head and put them to sleep. That way they'll use less oxygen.'

'Yes – '

'If I have to knock every single one of them unconscious to save oxy I'll do it. And you, too, Taynor Rafflans.'

'You would, too, you terran bastard.'

Rafflans went back and Hook said: 'I'll take over now, O'Steele. You get back and give Rafflans a hand.'

'But – '

'Jump! And breathe light.'

O'Steele jumped. And breathed lightly.

The hours ticked by as the mega kilometers were crossed through the emptiness of space. Outside this thin hull the galaxy flamed and coruscated away. Hook knew the heartlessness of that galaxy. He'd trade a sizeable proportion of it off right now for good sweet breathable air in here.

He felt muzzy.

He put the ship on auto and headed back to the passenger compartment.

Most of the people were silent, sitting or lying down, heads sunk on breasts, and some were already unconscious. The air felt thick on the tongue, metallic, unpleasant.

'How much longer, Hook?' asked Rafflans, in a voice fuzzy and strained.

'We'll make it, you Krifman bastard, never fear.'

'Remember, when we do, I'm going to rip you apart.'

'Sure. Now shut up and save oxy.'

Hook's head pained. Every now and then a knitting-needle of white-hot fire stabbed down into his frontal lobes, between his eyes. That expensive and sophisticated organic equipment he had inside his skull would be resonating like a campanile of best bronze clangers right now. He couldn't care less – he was going to take a long walk along the canal and find – what?

He shook his head. The fuzziness persisted. He'd been maundering then. He'd been treading familiar paths of his boyhood back on Earth when he'd wander along the canal bank to a lock and hope to earn a pek or two – one of the smallest units of money-metal – from pleasure-boat folk working through the lock.

He reached down under the throne and lifted the orange bottle. He twisted the seal and pressed the stud. A gust of oxy whiffed. The gas was compressed in there so that it was solidified; he aimed the blast to one side and sniffed its icy chill as it dissipated. At once he felt better. Most of the cylinder bulk was insulation. It would last half an hour at full throttle. He stowed it back.

Damned staccato way of living. He'd been looking forward to carrying on his life of ease down on Mergone. Damn disease! He just hoped Shaeel would for once have the sense to stop messing around and hurry out to Merfalla. The Hermaphrodite was so unpredictable. Then Hook chuckled. He knew he was himself a mass of contradictions . . .

He kept blasting the oxy off and the control section remained just tolerably sweet. Twice he went back to the passenger compartment. The second time almost everyone was lying listlessly and the card players just lay slumped over with their money-metal toppled beside them. Hook looked at it and smiled and stepped over it.

Rafflans looked up.

'It's worse than I thought, Hook.'

'Yes. One of the bottles must have been almost empty. Damned skinflint Copatec.'

Rafflans hoisted himself up. The air was still breathable with that tangy metallic taste; but by now the recycling gear must be pumping back nothing like a normal oxy-nitrogen mix. Hook didn't care to check just what percentage of oxygen was coming through.

'I'll come forward with you, Hook.'

'Suit yourself.'

Hook preceded the Krifman up the aisle. Fraulein Elterich smiled at him as he passed; but he ignored that. Myza was asleep, the yellow shirt twisted into creases each side of her breasts, the purple hair somehow ludicrous. In the control section Rafflans sniffed.

'I thought so, you cunning Terran bastard! You've got the emergency bottle up here.'

'Sure. And I'm keeping it. Someone has to be awake to bring this shuttle in.'

'I ought to – '

'Yes? You can have the bottle if you can bring the shuttle in, Rafflans.'

'You know goddam-well I can't!'

'So shut the face.'

Rafflans subsided. But the big Krifman was storing all this up. Hook wondered what stupid bravado had let him allow Rafflans up here. He pointed to the astrogator's seat folded up against the bulkhead and said: 'Sit there. I'll give you a squirt now and then. You might be useful.' He frowned. 'But first, get O'Steele up here. He's more use than you.'

'So help me, Hook, I'm going to – '

'Just do it, Rafflans, you clunkhead.'

Hook felt that spiralling, dizzying sensation and the feeling of pressure around his temples. He hauled the bottle out and squirted. Rafflans gulped greedily.

'We're like a couple of secret drinkers,' said Hook. 'Now go and get O'Steele.'

Rafflans went.

The luminous figures of the digital clock moved over with mocking slowness. Hook checked the air levels again. His calculations, indecently simple, indicated planetfall a bare ten minutes before the last of the oxygen gushed from the last cylinder. After that there would be residuals to come, and then a recycling that would pump less and less oxygen until, in the end, the stupid automotans would pump pure nitrogen and carbon dioxide, over and over again.

Say twenty minutes.

In that time he had to find somewhere to touchdown, and make that touchdown.

Once again he checked. No difference appeared in the picture.

O'Steele appeared in the control section.

'Lie down, son, and compose yourself.'

'If you want to fold your arms across your chest to save us the labour,' said Rafflans, croaking. 'That's IQ.'

Hook didn't laugh, and O'Steele looked crushed. He lay down. If he was needed, then Hook wouldn't be around.

The little pressurised orange ball squirted its last.

Hook didn't waste effort by throwing it away. He just let it drop down with a clank like the passing bell gone sour.

The air tasted like mouldy jam, furry and bitter.

A bleep chirruped from the console and a red light woke up and began to blink.

Hook looked for some time before he realised just what had happened.

He said: The detector has picked up a homing signal from Merfalla.'

'It can't have,' said Rafflans. 'The planet is uninhabited.'

'It has.' Hook pushed himself up and flicked on the lock-in. The signal continued, loud and clear.

'By the Great Salvor!' said Rafflans. 'It is!'

The shuttle nosed in toward Merfalla. She screamed in out of the starshot darkness, her deceleration calculated out to bring her neatly into orbit, her artificial gravity maintaining a steady point eight g inboard. Hook gripped on to his senses.

Down there, on this reputedly uninhabited planet, a radio was sending out a homing signal for incoming spaceships. He would take the shuttle down that beam of safety. He over-rode the normal orbital evolutions, cranked the shuttle around and sent her plunging down.

'We'll find out later – ' he said, and then stopped speaking. It was a struggle to breath now.

The screen picked up the curve of the planet, all hazy grey-streaked browns and blues, and then collapsed into itself as the horizon vanished and they were looking *down*.

The shuttle screamed down through atmosphere.

They rode the beam all the way.

The ground beneath fled outwards and off the sides of the screen with that sickening vertiginous sensation that seemed to whirl one's brain around inside one's skull. Yet they were falling straight down and the ground fled radially outwards.

That ground spouted up at them.

O'Steel was moaning. His face was an unhealthy colour, like the inside of a sewage pipe, and his tongue protruded between his lips.

Rafflans tried to hold on to the console, and collapsed. He fell down with his legs and knees buckling, sprawled on the deck. All manner of pains lanced through Hook's head. Everything was blurred. He had to hold this bucket up off the ground. His over-ride of the control meant she was now under his guidance. On manuals he must do it all. He had to haul her around before she hit the ground and burrowed on, falling to pieces, before she exploded.

He judged his moment.

Their speed was down now to barely supersonic.

He hauled her back and killed the speed and she flattened.

The beam held rock steady.

Now he could see a spaceport.

It jumped and bucked as he fought to hold the shuttle level. The ground was pouring past like a river.

Dust puffed ahead, and a wink of fire, and then a shape, broad and shining, sliding down from his right flank.

Another ship!

Yes. The ship for which this homing signal had been programmed! Another ship, heading on exactly the same vector as themselves, heading in for rendezvous with the spaceport. Two vessels – one, their tiny shuttle, and the other a monstrous spaceship, boring down to lock together in flame and smoke and destruction.

Chapter Four

So there were damned people on this planet, after all.

The homing signal was a relatively weakly powered beam and clearly intended only for local craft.

This planet might support life on the terminal edges of existence. Hook's awareness of himself and his surroundings picked up speed – significantly – but his whole attention now concentrated on the other ship arrowing in.

The ship let down following the same beam as themselves.

Hook let that concentration overlap into a fleeting thought that had the air been fully breathable here he could simply have blown a hole in the overhead and let the slipstream blow the fug away.

The screen lit up and a man's face showed, arrogant, heavy, accustomed to instant obedience.

Hook knew his sort.

'Get that heap out of Approach! You're interfering with scheduled landings here. Take Vector seven eight green and get out of the way!'

'Not likely,' said Ryder Hook.

The pictured face displayed all the symptoms of imminent seizure.

'Don't you understand, you cretin! A ship is landing *now*! And you're in the way! Get out of it – fast!'

'I'm making an emergency landing. I have seriously ill passengers aboard. We have been stranded in space – '

At subsonic speeds there was time to talk in sentences that were almost grammatically correct; unlike the staccato bursts of code-language necessary out in space. Hook's face felt congealed beneath the disguising facial-gel. His hair, a tasteful shade of iron-grey, flopped loosely on his scalp. He recognised the immense effort required to perform the most simple function.

'This is your last warning! Take your bucket out of here or we will fire on you.'

'Do that,' said Hook, 'And you'll burn your own ship.'

He wasn't going to argue. This time he was going to barrel in and let the fates of space – whoever they might be – look out for the other fellow.

The descending ship could be seen, now, a streak of silver with the sun of Tannenbar reflecting off that sleek hull.

Hook drove steadily on.

Converging courses – a fragile shuttle and a mammoth ship – closer and closer – the beam of the homing signal a scientific finger luring them on to destruction. Closer . . .

The face flicked from the screen.

Hook got the controls under his palms. His eyes swam with sweat and dizziness. Up ahead lay the dome and airlock and sweet refreshing air they could suck deeply into their lungs . . .

No other shipload of rubbernecking tourists or whoever would shove him out of the way now.

He delicately dipped the shuttle and then in a smooth zooming movement that brought the thermocouples chittering into life, he let her gain altitude.

The blast from the anti-aircraft batteries sited along the perimeter of the dome splashed liquid fire where the shuttle had been. Once more he could estimate the jink to fox ordinary fire-control radar. Once more. That once had to be enough.

He let the shuttle slide right down until she tore across the ground at deck level.

A blurring impression of speed, of a crazy whirl of colour and movement, with the dome shooting towards them and the opened valves which would enfold them in safety.

Hook slid the shuttle under the second blast.

The third would smack them cleanly and burn them.

Then he chuckled.

The other descending ship, her captain in no doubt that as was his right he would receive right of way, had continued to let down.

That colossal silver bulk settled along the line of the beam.

She showed for an instant, plain and distinct before him, directly in line.

Then the third blast lashed out.

That was a shortened blast. A chopped blast – a blast halted even as the finger pressed the button as the betraying radar warned – too late.

The third blast sprayed molten fire around the descending ship.

Her tail assembly blew away, instantly vaporised. She toppled, spouting fire. When she hit the shuttle screamed above her, buffeted by the shock, dipped, dived, streaked for the valve opening.

Hook didn't spare a thought for the savaged ship.

People would have been killed; but that wasn't his fault.

He whipped the shuttle into the opening and let her down and cut the power.

Inside he could hear only the useless susurration of the re-cycled nitrogen and carbon dioxide. He had to keep awake and to think.

He cracked the seals on the airlock and then tried to stand up from the pilot's throne and walk aft.

His legs wouldn't support him.

From the throne he triggered the door mechanism.

If the monkeys out there didn't close the airlock valves and flood the landing area with air – well, if they did not do that everything else had been a waste of time.

Hook knew they'd do it, though. They'd want to get their hands or their tentacles on the maniac who had brought a shuttle in and wrecked one of their ships.

Something trilled in the stinking atmosphere aboard the shuttle.

Hook sniffed.

Oxygen!

Fresh air welled in through the open airlock. Hook struggled up, fighting the nausea, keeping the vomit down, hauled himself into a shambling semblance of an upright posture.

'Now you bastards, come and get me,' he mumbled.

He could hear voices now, and the clink of metal, out there in this vast hangar-like space. The shuttle must look extra-ordinarily tiny, squatting in the centre of a pad designed for mammoth spaceships.

He caught O'Steele under the armpits and dragged him out of the way. Rafflans lay, his face orange and blue, his tongue thrusting past his teeth. Hook left him. He went back into the astrogation area and stripped off the facial-gel. He pulled off the iron-grey wig. He bundled them up with the stripper and stuffed them into a plastic bag along with the radio set he'd lashed-up. Holding the neck of the bag he walked down the aisle.

People were groaning and he could hear the snorting blurting of lungs grappling with the unfamiliar task of dealing with real oxygen again. He guessed some of those passengers would never wake up.

He yanked his bag from the rack and pulled out a flamboyant scarlet cloak with the black edgings. It had been made for him on Pantacles, and the smiling tailor of The Spaceman's Pit had told him that, yes, taynor, this style is all the rage in the galaxy now. Hook put the cloak on.

At least five men among the passengers wore garments of a similar cut and colour, with different bindings. He wouldn't look out of place whatsoever.

He sprawled out under a seat and flicked his lighter at the plastic bag.

The bag, his wig and the facial gel, the radio, whiffed into flame, which burned sullenly and blackly, greedily sucking oxygen needed elsewhere, burned and slaked and died into a brown gooey ooze.

Hook shoved that aside with the sole of his black boot and sprawled out in a more abandoned posture, an arm flung across his eyes, and waited to be rescued.

The beings who entered the shuttle and began removing the reviving passengers were Reakers.

Listlessly among the others, Hook was picked up and thrown over a broad scale-plated shoulder, and carried outside where art-grav clamps held the passengers suspended in midair in neat rows.

He hung there next to an Earthwoman of indeterminate age, whose fashionable glitter-clothes pulled around her revealing feet with one shoe between them. A mal was hoisted alongside Hook, one of the race of Homo mal with their chunky bodies and grimly forbidding faces with the high cheekbones and slanting eyes, the tubular ears, so characteristic of this race old in the galaxy. Hook looked down.

Only one human being appeared to be directing the Reakers.

This man – Hook felt fairly confident he was Homo sapiens – wore tight bright-blue clothes with an orange cloak, and he shouted in the intemperate way some humans assumed when giving orders to Reakers. The Reakers were what interested Hook most, for although he had met many exoskeletal races in the galaxy, he had never as yet to his knowledge tangled with a Reaker, and he found them fascinating.

Their exoskeletons had to be exceptionally thick and rigid in order to contain their bulk, for they stood all of a metre and a half in height. The uncanny item here that Hook found confirmed immediately was their uniformity. If one Reaker's flatly-domed skull rose more than a couple of millimetres higher than any of his comrades, no one would notice that. Bunched together they looked like a level pavement of cobble-stones. Their two arms projected rather sideways from slit-like orifices between breast and back plates, and their legs and feet depended from a pelvic-girdle that, not being endoskeletal, hung around the laminated base of their upper platings. Their faces bore short-stalked eyes, set wide apart, of ears no sign, slits for breathing and rat-traps of mouths that looked as though they could gnaw through metalloy and spit out the pips.

They were obedient to their masters, and they worked well – and they were nastily vicious if let off the chain.

Ryder Hook fancied he would have trouble with the Reakers.

They wore fancy curlicues acid-etched on their shells and bits and pieces of finery that included many feathers and imitation-jewelled straps and belts. Hook did not miss the over-size dis-gel guns they wore strapped above the articulated laminations between breastplate and thighplates.

'Bunch of intelligent lobsters,' he said.

The Earthwoman had recovered, breathing stertorously, and she started in screaming at once.

Strange how some folk couldn't always accept the profuse diversity of human shape throughout this teeming galaxy!

The process of bringing the passengers from HGL starship *Talcahhuano* back to life did not take long and soon they were floating along plastic-walled corridors to a rest centre. Hook had doubts that many econorgs would be represented down on this mystery planet of Merfalla; but he guessed that some quick-talking would establish mutuals between agencies to take care of all those people boasting wrist credit cards.

Hook was a galactic loner. He did not boast a wrist credit card.

He heard the human in the orange cloak yelling.

'Nowhere, you bunch of all-fired dolts! He must be some-where. He was distinctly seen and we have a record of the conversation. He has to be aboard somewhere.'

A Reaker whose orange shell bore more feathers and beads and straps than the others said: 'He is not aboard. Presence negative.'

Rafflans wandered over to Hook in the rest area, threading his way between the loungers and coffee tables. He smiled.

'They're looking for you, Hook.'

'I might have known your beady eyes wouldn't be fooled.'

Rafflans laughed. Everyone was very happy. They'd been saved from a hideous death, hadn't they?

'Your Tonota Eighty. I don't miss a gun's characteristics. And you still have that fool Jahnian's Krifarm model twelve in your thigh pocket.'

'I did not intend to fool you, Rafflans. Just these people.' He didn't wish to plead with a Krifman.

'That'll be all IQ. But it don't mean I'm not going to rip your arms and legs off, Hook, you Terran bastard, and wrap 'em around your scrawny terrestial neck.'

'You know, Rafflans, you great Krifman twit, I'm looking forward to that wrapping operation.'

Rafflans chuckled and flicked his thick thumb and finger for a service robot. The machine trundled across and Rafflans took the dish of steaming coffee that Homo sapiens had managed to inflict on the Krifmans as a subtle punishment. Hook took good honest tea, and relished it.

The processing of the rescued passengers went on, and none could give any coherent account of what had happened in the shuttle after they'd passed out. All they knew was that a Taynor Hook had been trying to bring them in.

'Was he like this?' and a photograph-cube of Hook would be studied, and a nod would follow, and: 'Yes, that's him.'

Soon the forensic sniffers would have his hair follicles and body-cell detritus, some of his wastes still in the air of the control section, all, neatly packaged up and ready for the computer. When matches were made with the survivors the only match that mattered would be the one that indicated that Ryder Hook, no matter what he looked like, was Ryder Hook.

Well, Hook had got out of tighter scrapes before. He had just to think what he was about, and –

And . . .

A tingling all along his organo-metal bones brought Hook quiveringly alive.

Really, fully, truly alive, as he looked at Rafflans he felt the thrilling, jumping all along his nerve-endings as they streamed billions of messages about his body, as his brain speeded up into a near-superhuman level of activity.

How he dreaded this experience!

How he craved and thirsted for this experience!

A Boosted Man had come close enough to him for his own half-Boosted Man metabolism to resonate with those diabolical frequencies. The moment was transitory. As quickly as the symptoms had crashed upon him they passed.

But for those few heart-beats Hook had been a Boosted Man – and the passing of the evil state left him hollow and withdrawn and grey, a husk.

'What the hell's got into you, Hook?'

'Nothing except a damn-fool Krifman!'

He was back on form again.

'This damn-fool Krifman has a wrist credit-card that says he's with ZZI. ZZI, Hook. There's no better econorg in this man's galaxy. Who are you with?'

Officials in orange uniforms were moving among the survivors now, with their computerised questions, and their probes for forged credit cards and all the rest. Hook grunted and hauled up the left sleeve of his tunic.

'I'm with me, Rafflans, that's who.'

Rafflans didn't grasp that.

'You? A loner? Haw!'

Rafflans laughed, delighted at the colossal stupidity of Hook attempting to cut his own course in the galaxy when, as every intelligent man knew, to be under the protection of a multi-system conglomerate was the only way to survive.

Hook spoke with a genuine sourness.

'There was a ZZI agency on Mergone, Rafflans, you great Krifman idiot. But here? On Merfalla? Did you even know there were *people* on this goddammed planet?'

'No – I – what the hell are you getting at, you sapiens ape?'

'Just that something screwy is going on.'

'I'm an executive with Krifarm – yes, that's why I know about weapons – and I'm not going to be fooled with, believe you me. I'll have whatever agency is down on this dump squeaking out over the parsecs so fast for ZZI their tails won't touch the ground.'

'You may be a big shot, Rafflans.' Hook spoke quietly. He couldn't tell this big hulking Krifman that wherever there were Boosted Men there was grief for ordinary decent humanity. The Boosted Men were out, for their own dark and twisted ends, to dominate as much of the galaxy as they could, which nonsensical concept sickened Hook. But he knew the Boosted Men meant to do it and, what was even more horrifying, they were capable of it. They called themselves the Novamen. They played for the highest stakes there were between the stars and all the rules were their own.

Hook finished as quietly: 'Just don't annoy these people. They might not like ZZI much.'

Such an idea struck Rafflans as absurd.

'We're a bigger econorg than – ' he began. One of the orange uniformed officials stood before them.

'No matter how large or important your econorg may be,' the official said in a voice that rasped with repetition. 'I'll say this once. Get over to the desk and deposit your weapons. Check them in carefully. Down here on Locus we do not recognise any econorg but one. So walk carefully.'

None – except the startling exception of Hook – had spoken to Rafflans like that in years and years. He gaped. Then: 'What the hell are you blatting about, terrestial ape! I'm an important – '

'Shut up and get over with the others.'

The Martian Mega looked enormous in the official's hand. It had leaped there from its holster, and only a Boosted Man could have seen it move.

Rafflans bristled and started to shout. Hook shoved him.

'Let's get over there and check our guns. You'll have your guts shot out otherwise, you Krifman fool.'

Rafflans just didn't believe what was happening to him. In the next couple of hours his weapons were taken from him, his money-metal was taken, he was stripped of his clothes and handed a pair of dun orange coveralls, he was given a swift physical, food was dished out on plastic-paper plates, a dismal meal, and he was herded with the other survivors into the capacious hold of a freight flier. All the time officials in the garish uniforms held guns pointed at him and the other survivors.

The man in the tight bright-blue clothes and orange cloak spoke to them.

'You have come to Locus and you will work. Conditions are good. If you attempt to escape, however, you will be punished. But I know you will not want to escape. You will now be taken to your centers of employment. *Move!*'

As he went out with Hook, Rafflans said: 'I just don't believe it! I don't believe it!'

Chapter Five

When they stepped out from the freight flier's hold on to a landing apron and saw about them the towers and blocks and complexes of an industrial city, the girl Myza spoke crossly to her friend Fraulein Elterich.

'They're punishing us, Anthea! It's all the fault of that horrible Hook man! He smashed up their spaceship and now they're punishing us!'

'I don't think so, Myza. Anyway, they'll catch Hook soon. You can't sit in a pilot's seat and not leave enough traces.' Anthea Elterich's brows drew down. 'Anyway, he saved our lives. I feel sorry for him.'

Myza sniffed.

'What sort of man is he, then? He's hiding among us. I don't know half these passengers – who would, when the ship carried over three thousand? I only met that nice Denis when we stopped aboard the shuttle.'

Denis, a man whose black hair shone with oil and ministrations, and whose chest tended to the concave rather than the convex, summoned courage enough to smile. Myza's purple hair had turned spotty under the washings, and some of its mousey brown showed through.

Hook stood to their rear, silently, listening.

Rafflans nudged him.

'If we turned you in, you chancroid, they might let us off.'

'You don't believe that, Rafflans. They've got an operation going on down here. It's secret. This planet is supposed to be uninhabited. Yet look at that industrial power!'

Rafflans moved his hand in Krifman contempt.

'ZZI wouldn't even notice a hundred units like this. But I grant you it's impressive enough, near-to, like this.'

They started forward under the threat of guns in the fists of brightly-uniformed guards. The cracked concrete showed weeds sprouting valiantly. The air, at least, under the dome shrouding the city smelled fresh. Outside, on the planetary surface, no doubt conditions were barely livable. You'd certainly be dead out there without protection of the kind afforded, not by an econorg, but by a spacesuit with full supplies.

The pavement changed to a pedway and the party sped on.

'It's mostly chemical engineering,' said Rafflans.

'Yes,' said Hook.

'I'll not turn you in, Hook. I don't want anyone else stealing the pleasure of tearing you limb from limb.'

'That's big of you.'

Hook had steered clear of the other survivors. He fancied his disguise had implanted a set impression on their minds, and now he had discarded it they just did not recognise him among the party where they did not know everyone. But he had the sneaking suspicion that if Myza or Anthea Elterich got a good clear look at him some stirrings of recognition would flicker. That Myza! She'd scream out at once and betray him to the guards on the instant.

They passed other workers going to and from the factories. Hook studied them. The people all looked ill. Their faces were gaunt and haggard. Their dull-orange coveralls were old and stained and ripped. And yet everyone walked the pedway, they laughed and joked and waved to one another. They behaved as if they were having a wonderful time.

The pedway glided on. Guards separated out parties detailed for different factories.

Myza let out a shriek of pleasure.

'Oh, Anthea! Look at the lake! And those yachts! There is good swimming there, and a restaurant where I know they'll serve best Ollindai – I always did love that drink.'

'Where?' said Anthea Elterich, and then: 'Oh, yes! How lovely the sunshine is, glinting off the yachts' sails.'

Hook stared in the direction in which the two girls were looking.

He could see a blank expanse of cracked and oil-stained concrete, and a blank concrete factory wall, and nothing else. Nothing remotely resembling a lake with scudding yachts met his astonished gaze.

'Those flowers,' said Rafflans, sniffing the pungent chemically-fouled air wafting from the factory. 'They smell sweet. I always did like flowers.'

Hook looked at the bulky Krifman.

He looked at Myza and at Anthea Elterich.

Mental manipulation had presented many a hazard in the turbulent past. It could still be found in out of the way places. This damned planet of Merfalla – or Locus as the guards down here called it – was well out of the way.

Hook cursed.

A small group of passengers hived off with those near Hook stood around a simple metalloy drinking fountain. The water gushing from the faucet looked slimy and green, nauseous. The people were filling tin cups and drinking it down, and Hook heard them exclaiming at the fine quality of the wine and spirits, and of how this place did a guy and a gal proud when it came to drinking dens. He sighed.

'Move along there, now, friends,' said a guard. He swung a rubber truncheon; but his gun was firmly holstered. 'There'll be plenty of drinking time when you finish your shift.'

The party moved on. Inside the first factory complex they were handed from overseer to foreman to robot to bench. The work they were required to do exactly fitted their capacities. Where a robot could do the work, then it would do so. Where a living intelligence was required, then an orange-coveralled human being, whether Homo sapiens or Homo mal or Krifman or any other of a bewildering variety of aliens, would do what was necessary.

Hook found himself at a bench supervising static robots in electronic-circuit assembly. He got through the work as fast as possible, adhering to the flow-charts on their flicker-screens. Overseers prowled. When he got out at the end of the shift he found Rafflans waiting, talking to Denis. The young man looked exhausted; but a look of anticipatory merriment flushed his thin features.

'It's very easy, the work. And tonight we're off to the yacht harbour and the lake. Then it's the restaurant – or maybe we'll have a barbecue on the beach. Myza is going to be very kind to me.'

'Lucky boy,' said Rafflans, expansively, smacking Denis on his narrow back. 'I'm for a spot of drinking myself.'

He saw Hook.

'Hey! Come on Alf. We're waiting.'

'Right with you,' said Hook.

They took the pedway to the lake where they soon palled up with a charming girl from Leostar, who had been working on Locus for some time and already had enough saved in her econorg's bank to set herself up in the cosmetic business she

36

planned to run back home. She had done exceedingly well to answer the advertisement and come here. The wages were exceptional and the conditions sumptuous. They had a pleasant sail, and then went through to the restaurant. Hook settled back in the softly padded chair and studied the menu.

Anthea Elterich had stared directly into his face as they had laughingly collided trying to fold and stow the sail, and if she had recognised him as Ryder Hook she had made no comment. For a fleeting instant Hook wondered why he should worry if she did know who he was. Rafflans called him Alf all the time now, as he remembered he had asked him to do, and everyone else called him Alf.

Alf was a nice name.

'Hey, Alf! How about the Dover Sole – never mind that it was caught here on Locus and never saw Old Earth in its flat little life!'

'Or the smoked salmon.'

'I'm for the truits de flota,' said Leona, the girl from Leostar. 'I'm not homesick; but I like to eat food I know is the best in the galaxy!'

'In that case,' said Rafflans, leaning confidentially across the bare shoulder of the girl where it gleamed with a healthy pink flush under the narrow glitter strap of her flung-out dress. 'You should try Krifman sucking-pig. Mmm! There's nothing like it on all the worlds.'

'Smokey bacon!'

'T-bone steak!'

'Oropsais of Dorven!'

'Bird pie – turkey and goose and peacock and all!'

Laughing, flushed, drinking exquisite wines, they ordered and the robots brought the food and they ate until they lay back, distended, fulfilled.

'What a meal!'

'Fantastic.'

'Brandy?'

Brandy it was for all except Hook. He drank tea.

'I'm the only civilised person here!'

'Philistine!'

They had to explain what philistine meant to the girl from Leostar and Leona laughed delightedly and said: 'Back home we call them walkers-near-the-ground.'

They all roared at the joke.

Surely, life was great!

Later that night Hook escorted Anthea back to the luxurious hotel in which they had been quartered, rent-free. He stood in her room, with its suspended-bed, its soft rug, the shower cubicle, the tv with currently a tele-drama miming away, casting lights across the room where the rosy lamps had been turned down. Hook stretched. He did not feel tired; just pleasurably fuddled.

Anthea let him kiss her.

She responded with a sudden abandon that made Hook feel that life could be very sweet, if you allowed it.

He pushed down the strap of her demure evening dress, of some greenly-clinging material that, for some odd reason, changed occasionally to an orange hue under the mingled glow from the lights and the tv. Her skin was very smooth and of that glorious golden colour thousands of years of mutual inter-breeding had brought to make wonderful the race of men and women.

She opened her mouth.

She was moist and warm and delicious and Hook let himself slide away and dive self-indulgently into the abysses of forgetfulness in passion.

Next morning he felt great and couldn't wait to get through the shift. His back ached a trifle, and that made him think he ought to take a work-out in the gym. He'd seen the lavish provision of expensive equipment, shining under the sun's rays, and he breathed in deep lungsful of air, fresh and bracing.

Yes, Anthea was a passionate little girl and he had to keep in shape. They were going to the opera as soon as they had eaten after the knocking-off whistle, and then – well, who knew? The whole gaudy playground of the city was open to them. Locus was one real pleasure centre, there was no doubt about it.

Mind you, all this fun and pleasure and plenty was entirely due to the beneficial influence of science. Science had brought the peoples of the galaxy through some incredible problem times in the past. There had been that period when the many different races of the galaxy had been shooting off into space, ftl drives had proliferated, contacts were being made, trivial territorial wars, even, had been fought. But now the galaxy boomed along and everyone had a share in the security and wealth. Oh, yes, there were wars, still, when some primitive race suddenly decided they must carve out a so-called empire among the stars for themselves. There were still conflicts. But the multi-system conglomerates would step in to protect their investments. No sane person would stand for an interstellar war. The upside-down notion that a 'Galactic Empire' was anything more than a drug-dream had long since gone.

Galactic Empires were kid's daydreams in the real galaxy.

Hook's thoughts turned in upon themselves. He was called Alf. He was meeting a beautiful girl with grey eyes tonight, Fraulein Anthea Elterich, and she would be kind – very passionately kind – to him. He licked his lips. She'd been all over him, her golden body bare and glorious, warm and sensuous, demanding all that he joyed to give her.

Why, then, should his thoughts maunder on silly children's ancient nonsenses like Galactic Empires?

Back eighty centuries or so on Old Earth the benighted fools then had used up all the fossil fuels in an almighty spending splurge. Then they'd had to scrape around for alternative sources of energy. Oh, yes, they'd found them; but that had been little credit to the businessmen or the politicians or the insatiable consumers. Science had come in and baled out Homo sapiens then. The same pathetic story had been enacted on a thousand planets around the limb of the galaxy – a million.

Old Earth had been invaded by those crazy six-armed nuts from Carpella. Earth had dominated a mighty commonwealth of suns herself, had dwindled in power, to lie forgotten and neglected. The continental masses had shifted. Old Earth had become a garden planet, and then a city-wide planet serving a million solar systems, and then had lodged herself into her own niche within the other planets and races of the galaxy so that a man – a Homo sapiens – of Earth became just another of the life forms living in the galaxy shoulder to shoulder. Population pressures had become insupportable, and it had dwindled finally to a desert-planet. Another race lived on Earth, now, in harmony with Homo sapiens. The two worked together. Changes and upheavals had gone on – and still, through them all, a straight and direct line of knowledge existed between the earliest civilisations of Earth and the present day. Hook dated his own birth at the First of January, in the year One Hundred nought one – ten thousand and one, the first day of the hundred and first century.

There were many and many forms of reckoning time and calendars multiplied in the galaxy. But you couldn't even conceive of a date like that on which Ryder Hook had been born if you didn't have continuity.

He wandered gently from the gym to meet Anthea.

Just why his thoughts had strayed down those old yet fascinating paths he couldn't say, especially when there were ripe red lips and grey eyes, golden limbs and golden breasts, firmness of flesh and healthy lust waiting for him. He was a museum nut, he acknowledged that. It was a vice.

Again he paused.

Something was troubling him and he didn't know what it was and that, despite that it was all of a piece for Alf, was insupportable for Ryder Hook.

Anthea ran up and kissed him and they went into the opera house together. She looked stunning in a white two-piece that displayed her long golden legs. Her hair shone. Her eyes danced. She was a most delectable piece of girlhood.

After the concert – Hook had strangely forgotten the music the instant they stepped from the marble stairway – they decided a drink and a meal would fortify themselves for the night's labours of love.

In the restaurant Hook waved to Rafflans and Leona, and they waved back and came over.

'Hey, Alf, you missed a great race! That scarlet number one rocket fairly burst the guts of that mauve number six! Boy, you should've seen the smoke and heard the bang!'

'Maybe that's what was wrong with the music.'

Leona looked excitingly sexy in a low-cut dress of some semi-transparent gauze that revealed just how alike and yet how dissimilar her figure was to an Earth girl's. Anthea laughed a lot. They drank champagne. On the salaries they were earning, even with the savings they were pumping into their accounts with their econorgs' banks, they could afford to live very high off the galactic hog indeed.

'Say, Alf,' whispered Rafflans, leaning close and sliding his eyes lecherously towards Leona. 'If you've never been up happy-trail with a girl from Leostar – you know nothing!' His eyes popped. 'Man, can she!'

'I'll believe you, Rafflans. But I'm satisfied, thank you.'

'You low-down scheming dirty-dog! That Anthea's a nice girl!' Rafflans looked puzzled. 'Say, Alf. Wasn't I going to knock your head off and wrap your arms around your neck?'

'You what?'

'Something like that. Look – there's that crazy bitch Myza and old pipe-stem himself. Hey! Come on over!'

Myza looked devastating too, in a dress that was not so much a see-through gown as a birthday suit with patches. Denis was drooling. Hook allowed himself a good look, too, for although nudity between the sexes was nothing in these enlightened days, nakedness and nudity still retained their old yin and yang appeal. Anthea nudged him.

'You'll make Myza blush.'

'Never!' roared Rafflans. He helped himself to a galaxy-sized portion of strawberries and whipped-cream, with a lagoon of brandy for good measure. 'She'll cut you dead if you don't stare on her beauties.'

'I'll allow that,' said Ryder Hook, stuffing strawberries and cream into his mouth with a silver spoon. He reached for the champagne. By dear Old Dirty Berti Bashti! Life was sweet!

Around them the sumptuous restaurant buzzed and hummed with men and women and aliens in beautiful clothes all eating and drinking. Laughter rang on the scented air. Discreet lighting slid golden gleams on warm flesh, cast star-sparkles into amorous eyes, reflected from jewellery and silver. The whole atmosphere was one of leisure and pleasure and hedonism carried to rarefied heights of sensual luxury.

Hook lifted his silver spoon of strawberries and cream and looked at Anthea, whose lithe and voluptuous figure sat so closely to his on the padded gilded chairs under the roseate lamps.

A trilling tingling started along his spine. The silver spoon vibrated. By the Great Salvor, as they said, Anthea could set a man's very blood on fire!

The thrilling persisted. A silver fog obscured his vision. He felt his bones rattling inside his skin. He looked at the cheap plastic spoon in his hand and the nauseous slop dripping from it to fall into the scummy pool in the cracked dish on the filthy table. Anthea was cuddling up to him, laughing. Her dull orange coverall was stained with grease and dirt. Leona's coverall had been ripped down from the neck and through rents and rips in the coarse material he could see her skin, smeared with dirt. And Myza – Myza sat there in the wreck of a coverall that was held together by little more than the threads. Her body showed bruised and scratched, with oily marks grimy upon the skin.

He saw the battered metalloy cup with the foul water scumming the rim, he saw Anthea lift it to her lips and drink, and heard her say: 'This champagne is the best I've drunk!'

And he knew.

He was no longer Alf.

Ryder Hook knew.

Around him men and women and aliens were sitting laughing and eating and drinking at filthy plastic tables. They ignored the rusty walls of the derelict shed in which they sat. Harsh actinic-lights glared down from shadeless holders. The whole place stank.

The filth in his dish nauseated Hook.

But he sat there.

He just sat there.

A man was passing through the shed between the rickety tables, a man in a black tunic and black breeches. He walked with the confident spring of the supremely self-assured.

And Hook sat and watched as Anthea shovelled squalid artificial food into her lovely mouth. He watched as she drank scummy water from a cracked tin mug.

Ryder Hook sat and watched and dare not spring up and dash the mug from her lips.

And yet – he dare not remain here like this. For if he did the illusion of the sumptuous restaurant would return and he would once more taste strawberries and cream and champagne.

And he would be trapped, then, perhaps for ever until he died from the exhaustion writ clearly on every person's face.

For, he could not risk the chance that another Boosted Man might walk through here and so release him from this hypnotic spell.

Chapter Six

Anthea put her arm around his waist, laughing, carefree, and said: 'Come on, Alf, darling! Let's dance.'

Couples were rising from the crazy chairs and beginning to dance one of the old-time high-kickers-and-stomps across the littered floor between the rickety tables.

Hook couldn't hear any music.

But Anthea dragged him up, laughing, tapping her feet already to the invisible ghostly beat.

'You old lead-tail! Get with it.'

'Sure, sure, Anthea,' he said, and stood up. People were dancing now, gaily, recklessly, their thin arms and legs jerking in the rhythms of unheard music.

The man clad all in black had reached halfway across the untidy room and Hook saw his face, saw the irritation and contempt writ large there, the distaste.

Well, these hypnotised workers were an unsavoury bunch. The wonder was that they could walk at all, given their physical condition, let alone dance. Hook understood they were under the compulsion of whatever system of mind-control was in use here. No one had electrodes affixed to their scalps that Hook could see and he felt sure, anyway, that a far more modern method than that clumsy old system of control would be in use.

The power that could chain them to a set of hallucinations and drive them into accepting squalor as luxury could also as easily galvanise their muscles and will-power into the effort of acting up to the requirements they thought necessary. There was waste here, intolerable waste. When a man fell down, half-dragging his partner with him, in the last stages of exhaustion, his companions laughed and crowed and called him a drunken slob. The man himself laughed, too, weakly, struggling to stand up. He was carried outside, still chuckling and waving arms like pipe-cleaners, firmly convinced that he was happily befuddled and with no idea whatsoever that he was dying.

The Boosted Men were running this planet they called Locus.

They'd find more workers in the galaxy, men and women anxious to earn big salaries. They'd use them mercilessly and discard them. Not a pek of the money would ever find its way into the dupes' bank accounts.

The man in black passed on and he avoided the gyrating dancers with a contemptuous ease that infuriated Hook.

'You're not dancing, Alf!'

Anthea pressed close, her arms were about his neck, her sweet face so grimed in dirt close to his. He could smell the stale sweat of her body, the stink of oil and chemicals on her. That compounded stench had seemed sweet female perfume only moments ago.

'Sure, Anthea, sure.'

He took her in his arms and began to kick and stomp and she chided him with: 'Keep to the music, you big ape!'

He didn't say: 'There is no music.' He couldn't.

That man in black was a Novaman. If he saw any of those dupes behaving in any way differently from the programmed instructions flooding in on them through the pervasive air his suspicions would be aroused. At once. Hook knew the speed of Boosted Men. Wasn't he half a Boosted Man himself?

Half a Boosted Man . . . A petty, stupid, destroying half . . .

The man in black passed on and Hook heard the thin and ghostly strains of an orchestra. He smelled sweet scent from the cleavage between Anthea's breasts. He saw a laughing girl in a brilliant glitter dress a a table lift her glass goblet and saw the champagne bubbles rising and bursting, he saw and he smelled and he heard – and absolute panic hit him.

He fairly ran Anthea after the Boosted Man.

The music died, the stinks returned; the girl sipped scummy water from a cracked tin mug.

By Dirty Berti Bashti!

He daren't let the Boosted Man get too far – and the range over which this resonance between a full Boosted Man and himself could strike up the buried half of his new nature and so turn him into a fully-developed Boosted Man himself varied unpredictably. He knew that in space the resonance could operate over many millions of kilometres. Onplanet it might remain fully functional over several kilometres, or it could waver and die within the confines of a room. Much depended on the programming of the Novaman who set up these thrilling and wickedly lascivious currents in his own body.

44

He danced and pranced and dragged Anthea after the man in black.

'Alf! What the hell are you playing at? Can't you dance all of a sudden – ?'

'Let's go outside, Anthea,' he said. His voice thickened. Anthea took the obvious reading of that, and she threw her head back so that the long line of her throat showed, golden and vulnerable, and she laughed and hugged him and they ran outside into the star-spangled night together.

Hook stared about. The Boosted Man walked rapidly towards a massive and lightless block over a double-strip pedway. A guard patrol skimmed past in a flier, and the orange-clad men inside flicked up a salute which the Boosted Man acknowledged by a half-raised hand. Hook watched.

His powers were enormous, phenomenal, frightening, when he was Boosted. He was Boosted now, thanks to that bastard in the black comic-opera uniform. He could see clearly in the darkness. The Boosted Man entered the dark foyer and Hook felt the trilling along his organo-metal bones die and quiver reluctantly away.

He held on to himself.

That building . . .

As he watched it subtly transformed itself from a mere massive block into the familiar shape of Central Records.

'What are you going there for Alf, at this time of evening? No one ever goes there.'

That was true. Hook realised the hypnotic compulsion kept the workers away from Central Records.

So that meant he had to get in.

Had to.

For Anthea's bedraggled orange coverall slid and changed into her exciting white two-piece, her body-stink altered into alluring perfume, and music floated out into the night from the sumptuous restaurant at his back.

Anthea pressed herself to him, demanding.

Hook shook his head, a useless gesture. If he simply ran into that building now – the restaurant and the dance and the fine wines and lavish food called to him. He clawed to keep his sanity. He was lost if he forgot. The chance that a Boosted Man had walked through – the chance that that might never happen again – he had to hang on – and yet Anthea was very sweet, clinging to him, her ripe lips lifted in invitation, her body close to him, warm and luscious and immensely exciting . . .

How long had he been a walking zombie under the influence of these womb-regurgitant Novamen's hypnosis?

Surely by now they must have processed out the forensic findings? They'd have come snooping around for him, to take him back to be punished for smashing up their spaceship, and they'd laugh as he underwent the refined agony of a discipline cell. He'd been living very high off the galactic hog just lately – all in his own imagination, of course – and if he knew the Boosted Men at all and their malevolent way of carving their kilogramme of flesh with blood as well into the bargain he knew they'd never allow him even those illusionary pleasures. It could be they needed workers pretty desperately for the project they had going on down here on Locus. They were clearly working all out in order to meet a deadline, although just what it was they were manufacturing Hook had no idea. He was merely a small cog, a human supervisor, adding his quota of work to the general output.

The patrol flier circled and returned. With the last few tattered remnants of sanity left to him, Hook saw the armoured body and armoured transparent hood, the hard-faced men inside, their guns, their paralysis weapons, all the viciousness of efficient control.

The sergeant leaned out as the flier hovered. He wore a blue helmet and face mask and he looked dangerous, as though he liked nothing better than knee-cap smashing and skull-breaking.

'Everything all right, sir?' The goon spoke quietly, formally, very correct.

Hook nodded. He managed to get out: 'Sure, officer – '

The outlines of the flier fuzzed. It changed. He was looking at a normal open flier patrol car, unarmoured, with the friendly policemen inside with fat comfortable faces, and not a gun in sight. They wore casual uniform clothes, with cloth uniform caps, and they were only too anxious to help.

'Sure,' said Alf, the electronics-robot-supervisor. 'Just getting a breath of fresh air.'

'It really is sweet tonight.' The goon looked at Anthea and chuckled. 'Sweet is right. Good evening, sir.'

And the flier trundled off.

He had to remember something – something important.

But Anthea was clinging to his arm and gazing up into his face and the warmth and closeness of her figure, the voluptuous-

46

ness of her body pressed close to him, dizzied him. He licked his lips.

'Do you want to go back to the dance?'

'Not really.' She giggled.

'Let's go to your place, then.'

He watched as her white two piece moved with her breathing, watched as her hips swung, watched as her long exciting legs slithered nylon one against the other. They walked along the night-flowered streets, savouring the air, walking in friendly fashion to a rendezvous with passion and frenzy.

Yes, it was good to be alive on Locus.

But – a nagging doubt hung across this bright good life, and Hook shook his head uselessly again and wondered why this black spider-web should spin itself across his pleasure.

Later that evening, after Anthea, he walked back to the hotel room that gave him such splendid service, still pondering. Now, just what was it that had so upset him before Anthea's blandishments had driven every other thought from his confused mind?

He knew that at all times he must remember he was not a superman.

He had to remember that, to save his own sanity and self-respect, such of it as he still wanted to keep; but why?

He had been used all his life to walking in the shade, as a loner and an outcast, one who owed no allegiance to any multi-system conglomerate, one who would be trodden flat unless ready always to preserve identity and pride.

Pride?

For Ryder Hook?

That didn't make sense, either. That was just a laugh.

But he wasn't a superman.

He wasn't even a failed superman – one of those mythical lay-figures so beloved of the tv and tridi entertainment industry.

He had once belonged to RCI, one of the most formidable of multi-system conglomerates with its main headquarters on Earth and with tentacles of power and finance reaching out over the stellar abysses. RCI. Rocket Consortium Interstellar. They'd – what had they done? They'd thrown him out, hadn't they? After he'd been selected for the new Powerman Project. Yes. He'd had scientific wizardry practised on him, so that some of his body cells and molecules had been replaced by metalloy structures. He was partially metallic. Well, that had been to equip him for work on a heavy-gravity planet. But he'd failed. He'd been thrown out. His father had died in some freak accident, no one would tell him any details, and his mother had died, and his younger brother and sister had taken off into the galaxy and he hadn't seen them in years.

Then he'd been with Earth Armed Services Intelligence as Sergeant Jack Kinch. But he'd left EAS, too, hadn't he? The most notorious assassin in the galaxy – and he'd become himself again, plain Ryder Hook, galactic adventurer, seeking to keep himself alive and have a crust of bread and perhaps a little pleasure on the side.

So who was Alf?

Hook was aware that he was a man of contradictions, and he bemoaned his vices. One vice was that he couldn't stand a fool, and therefore he tried to treat idiots with a special consideration he carried as his own personal cross. But he was acting as the complete fool now. Here he was, down on Locus, a fine planet, working at a good job with electronics, a subject of which he knew he was a master, earning a good wage, socking the cash away in the bank, having a whale of a time – so why these doubts, these vague and formless fears? What was nagging him?

He had to get into Central Records.

Yes. This silly unease had something to do with Central Records.

A call on the ident plate and Rafflans' voice heralded the Krifman bearing drinks. He plonked a bottle of best Ollindai on the table and beamed at Hook.

'Myza recommended this, Alf, and it is really something. Sup up, lad! The night's young.'

The bottle was old and cobwebby, of an exciting dark ruby colour, with a long spout-neck, and the encrusted labels promised the vintage had been plucked and trodden and matured all of a hundred years ago. A hundred years terran. Locus had a – what was it? – a fifty terran-hour day and night cycle.

'Myza treating you well, Rafflans?'

Rafflans pulled the stopper. He chuckled. 'I'm doing all right. I bought her a pearl necklace today and tomorrow she gets it and I get my reward.' The bottle banged satisfactorily. 'Champagne Ollindai! Superb!'

Rafflans poured and they drank.

'Have you ever been in Central Records, Rafflans?'

'No. Of course not. No reason to. I know what I know. I'm –

hey! Easy up, lad! At least let me even with you.' For Hook had drained the glass at a gulp.

'I thought you were with Krifarm?'

'Yes, of course. ZZI and Krifarm, the best combination in the whole galaxy. Well, I *was* as I said. I left 'em, though, didn't I? Came to Locus. Well, no matter. I'm here and you're here and the girls are here. Drink up, Alf!'

Hook squinted at the Krifman. They fancied themselves in the galaxy. A Krifman was a bad enemy and a good friend. They were always a cut above themselves, though, thinking they were the Great Salvor's specially created lot. At least, Hook thought so – he fancied that of the fantastically varied religions of the galaxy, Earthmen and Krifmans shared the same one. That was old, too . . .

'Have you ever seen a dynaman, Rafflans?'

'Yes. The agency tried to persuade me to become one, once; but I told them later on, when my own legs give out. Why?'

'Oh, nothing. I'm due early on the electronics bay tomorrow – that's today, already. You're on weapons, I take it?'

'Well, of course!' Rafflans drank again. The Champagne Ollindai was good, no doubt of that. 'Weapons I know. I had a dinky little Krifarm energy-junior when I was nine. Could vapourise all the plastic cups you could throw up, snap, snap, snap! Guns and me, Alf, go together.'

'And a Tonota Eighty?'

Rafflans laughed. 'That rubbish! A Krifarm model twenty! That's what I'm turning out now, beauties. A Tonota Eighty's a kid's gun compared to them.'

'Model twenties. That's interesting.' Hook was fumbling towards some line of thought whose origins he couldn't trace but whose outcome was all-important. 'I've always liked the Martian Mega.'

'We-ell,' said Rafflans, pursing his lips, looking judicial, balancing his glass on his knee. 'A fine gun. Yes, a great gun. Y'know, Alf, we can neurally and electronically fix a little weapon to our wrists, and it'll come shooting out when we trigger, and do the job for us. But I like the feel of a big gun in my fist.'

'I know.'

'Martian Mega, eh? Very potent.'

'And the Terran Pacifier?'

'Well, we're talking about guns the ordinary man can buy,

aren't we, Alf? I've never seen a Terran Pacifier.' He sounded most disgruntled about that.

'Stick to the Krifarm jobs, Rafflans. They're fine.'

'Who says they aren't?'

Hook sighed. 'Time for bed, Rafflans. Work in the morning.'

'Yes, yes, let me finish my drink. That opera you and Anthea saw – any good? I've never seen anything to beat the opera the Krifman Company put on – ' He rambled on about opera and ballet, while Hook sat trying vainly to remember what opera he and Anthea had seen, trying to bring back a fragment of melody, a strain of song, and failing. That was strange.

This was all bound up with this obsession that he must get into Central Records. He wasn't in the least tired. Sex seldom fatigued him. He wasn't tired and he wanted to break into Central Records; but he had a shift in the morning and he ought to get his sleep . . .

Damned odd situation.

When at last Rafflans left, nursing the last Ollindai in the bottle, Hook thoughtfully half-closed the door and stood, his head bowed, pondering.

If only this fuzziness in his head would go away!

It was difficult to think straight.

Thoughts and concepts poured disjointedly into his brain. There was Anthea, golden and glowing and exciting, pirouetting enticingly before him beneath the roseate lights. There was the electronics bay with the robots busy and the harsh actinic-lights gleaming down on assemblies whose function he could only guess at – something to do with remote-control of inter-diction of neural cell-endings and synapses so as to produce a desired effect. There was the yacht harbour and the lake beyond and the brilliant sails scudding across the blue water. There was the restaurant and the sumptuousness of food and drink and good conversation and dancing and music. Opera? Very funny he couldn't recall the opera, not a single snatch of a line.

Well, if he was to get a decent night's sleep and be fit for work in the morning he'd have to go and see what was so important about Central Records.

He didn't particularly want to go.

But he knew dismally that if he didn't go he'd never sleep.

Funny thing was, his hand dropped to his belt as he went out, as though he carried a holstered gun.

Now, who would need a weapon on so peaceful and friendly a planet as Locus?

Chapter Seven

Hook walked out of the hotel and into the star-shot night. Quietness breathed over the city. Lights scattered enough radiance for him to see the outlines of the buildings reaching into the cloud-wrapped confines of the dome. Outside the dome – hell! Why think about a place he would never see. The weather controllers would have to do something about that concentration of condensation up there soon. These artificial environments always insisted on acting by natural laws and forming clouds. If precipitation set in before a warning could be issued there'd be red faces at Weather and a few tart reminders of economic efficiency from the econorg bosses here.

He walked firmly for he had a purpose, however uncongenial such a purpose might be. Only a few people were about. The time was nearly an hour past midnight when the shifts changed. Well, if anyone tried to get in his way and stop him, he'd – he'd – why, he'd just have a friendly chat and no doubt they'd offer him a drink and they'd have a guzzle and a yarn and then, when the man had gone, he could proceed with finding a way into Central Records.

Strange how, for a moment there, as he'd thought of someone accosting him, his hands had bunched up into fists as if by habit.

Fists were never used on Locus. No need. Everyone was always friendly and pally and everyone was always having a good time.

He saw a drunk lying in the angle of wall and pedway and, smiling, Hook shifted him into a more comfortable position. The man wasn't very heavy; but Hook knew that he possessed incredible strength, luckily enough, and so he made no comment.

'Thanks, pal,' said the man in a husky voice.

The bottle at his side lay empty.

'Sleep it off, friend. You'll have a head in the morning if you don't take a kill-'em pill.'

'Certainly – will do.'

The drunk's voice slurred and he slumped, completely out.

Hook walked on, chuckling.

Central Records bulked above him and for a moment he considered turning back. But this silly nagging doubt drove him on. Something had been programmed inside his skull to make him do a certain thing and until that course of action had been completed, Ryder Hook knew well enough he'd get no rest.

His thoughts were of Anthea and the smooth golden curve of flesh between hip and waist as she lay on her side, her arms reaching for him, voluptuous, demanding, always coming back for more. Central Records – what on earth had got into his head to make him do a mad thing like this, going in where no one else ever bothered to go? Anthea – that's where he should be going. She'd be ready for him again before they went on shift. The thought braced him. He just had to get in here somehow – three or four of the enormous entrance doors were open – and find out if this itch in his head would go away. Then he would be free to go to Anthea.

He walked up the marble stairs. The doorway he had selected was the middle of the three. Its doors were of bronze, with golden bolt-heads worked into fantastical designs. Fluoros cast green and orange lights down, mingling and reflecting from the marble floor. His footsteps were loud and ringing in the foyer.

To one side a bank of elevator doors with their antigrav shafts indicated access to the higher storeys. To the other side extended the long counter where enquiries into records might be made. Only a cleaning robot was in view, chugging around with vacuum and mop, squeaking, spraying, taking no notice of him.

Well, now he was in. So what? But the itch still wouldn't go away.

It was all IQ so far. Yes, and very strange that he should be standing here, one foot half-raised like a loon, and still be absolutely unsure why he had come here, what had made him, what the hell he did next.

A light flashed on the centre elevator indicator. It clicked downwards, running speedily from floor fifty to floor thirty. It stopped there. Hook scuffed his foot on the gleaming marble floor and looked around uneasily, and watched as the light flickered on down past floor twenty.

He still couldn't work out what he *was* doing here.

The answer hit him so that he almost vomited all over that beautiful marble floor – only the floor was not marble. It was dull stained concrete, cracked and undulating, and the cleaning robot made no impression on it at all, old and worn-out and inefficient as it was. The gravshaft light winked down to the foyer level, and Ryder Hook understood as the tingling thrilling surged all along his bones again and trilled in his nerves and sent the blood dancing through his veins, he knew that a Boosted Man was coming down in that elevator.

He knew where he was, what he was and why he was here.

When he'd seen the Boosted Man disappear into Central Records and known he could not follow then, he'd implanted a signal in his mind, an imperative that would not let him rest until he had gone once more to Central Records.

All that old pals' act! The drunk he had seen outside was a man, dying alone and exhausted, shattered by the labour forced on him by the Novamen, and debauched by the hallucinatory pleasures that kept him in line and rendered this unspeakable life possible.

The elevator grille slid aside and light spilled across the concrete. Hook made himself scarce in the shadows.

'And remember, Welson,' the man in black was saying in a high hectoring voice as he stepped out. 'Your production curve is flattening again. If you can't handle the quotas I can find someone who can.'

'They'll swing up again, novir, that I promise. We have a new intake of workers due – '

'Just see to it. I'm not interested in excuses.'

'Yes, novir.'

Hook grimaced, a most unlovely sight in the shadow. A novir was of high rank among the Novamen. He'd have to take this beauty fast. He was now, in proximity to a Boosted Man, perfectly capable of walking across the floor and taking Welson's neck in his fists and dealing with the overseer. Welson would never see or know what hit him. Boosted Men moved *fast* when they wished.

But this novir could see, just as Hook, when in Boosted condition, could see him moving at the fantastic velocities of the Boosted Men.

Now the novir walked at slow speed out through the open doorway. Hook had to follow, this time, or lose again this evil power he craved for and loathed. And yet – and yet this over-seer Welson was not affected by the general hypnosis. The guards did not see and hear the phantom sights and sounds that kept the workers in dazed euphoria.

There had to be a scientific answer.

The novir was outside the door. Hook reared up and at fast speed whipped across the concrete. At this enhanced speed Welson remained in the act of turning to re-enter the elevator. Hook checked, studied the man. Ah! There – in his left ear. Hook inserted fingers that were not at all gentle and pulled out the plug. It was a tiny artefact, no bigger than a ladybird; but it would be packed with sophisticated electronics. Hook stuck it inside his left ear. He could still hear perfectly well.

Mind you – the guards would be controlled, also. They were not Boosted Men. They would have a control device incor-porated that would keep them mercilessly in line.

The power of the crystal-resonances from the Boosted Man flowed through Hook. As always, he felt wonderful. He knew the drug-like power conferred on Boosted Men, why they in-tended to hold on to their power and increase it in the galaxy no matter who was smashed in the process. But that very interflow of power gave him now the opportunity of working in speed time. He whipped the little ladybird plug out and went to work on it. All the time Welson's foot slowly let down to-wards the entrance to the grilled elevator opening.

Those famous black boots of Hook's he'd been allowed to keep – how could the overseers know what he had hoarded in there? – yielded up micro-tools for the job. In speed time his fingers worked with a fluidity of motion that gave him exquisite pleasure. He opened up the plug bypassing the booby trap, working so fast the fuse had no time to fire, being careful, though, and read all there was to be known, recognised what a devilish little gadget this was, ripped out the circuit that chan-nelled incoming signals into the wearer's ear, re-assembled and stuffed the plug back.

He ran for the door not quite fast enough to set his clothes on fire, and Welson had scarcely stirred.

Welson was moving in normal time. Every reflex animating Ryder Hook operated in speed time.

The novir in the fancy black tunic and breeches walked slowly towards the flier park.

His Boosted ears would pick up Hook's movements long before Hook could charge him and he'd switch into fast time instinctively. A gun would appear – and exit Ryder Hook.

He had to use his super-efficient brainpower to work a way out of this fix, for he was just completely incapable of letting well alone and slinking off to leave the Boosted Man untouched. When you couldn't fight your way out, you had to trick your way out. The old flung stone wouldn't fool the Novaman.

Then Hook smiled. Use the weapons of the Boosted Men's hypnosis against them!

Lovely!

He stepped jauntily out on to the street, moving in normal time, stuck his hands into his trousers' pockets, started up an unmelodious song, and staggered off down the street.

He was just another poor doomed worker of Locus, living in an artificial paradise.

He knew the hypnosis was a projection, and not drug-induced. In connection with its programme a command had been incorporated that said the workers would never see a Boosted Man as he walked among them. Only a Boosted Man's own powers could overcome that quality of mind control.

Hook rolled on, singing, reeling about, not acting the drunk; but acting an exhausted worker imagining himself to be drunk.

There might be spy eyes everywhere. He could be under observation right now. He tended to doubt it. The flier park was out of the general area where workers congregated, and, of course, that was a suspicious fact in itself.

The Boosted Man half turned; but Hook resolutely ignored him and rolled on, warbling away about Sultry Susy Shorthouse and her Sirian Sexy Sextet. It was a good old space-song.

He came abreast of the novir.

He sped into fast time, saw the incredulous incomprehension on the Boosted Man's face, reacted to the immediate and devastating Boosted reaction, got his knee into the man's groin, chopped him hard, kicked him in the face as he went down, stomped his head in as he lay there. Hook knew Boosted Men. They were extraordinarily hard to kill. Even then the novir got a hand to Hook's foot and almost wrenched it off. And the grey brain cells and bright blood spatted across the concrete.

Hook had no time to lean back, sagging, gulping for breath.

A Boosted Man's skull had sufficient metallic elements organically welded into it to make it into an armour-plated ball. Hook's filthy orange coverall was twisted and ripped and from the condition of the clothes of the people here it was quite clear the Novamen wasted nothing on replacements. They in general let their workers keep their own footwear if they were tough enough to save supplying a more tricky item of apparel. Hook's famous old black boots had done their trick. But for them he'd be struggling with this novir still.

Hook was well aware that a good few thousands of years ago the cult of the Black Boot had arisen, with deep psychological symbols attached thereto – it was a similar occurrence to the cult of the Denim Windcheater – but that was all in the past. Here and now his black boots were worn for severely practical purposes having nothing to do with sadism and slavery – although, come to think of it, smashing in the head of a Novaman would be considered sadism by another Novaman. By any normal standards of the galaxy it was like nipping a louse between finger and thumb.

As Hook had said to Ed Malcom, that time: 'You don't like killing and neither do I. But I don't have your noble will-power, Ed, your honourable spirit of integrity. I'm at base a weakling when it comes to having my head shot off. If someone tries to kill me, Ed, I'll stop him, and if he gets himself killed in the process, then that's his fault. You can go on and be the noble sacrifice for principles' sake. If I can I'll drop a few flowers on your grave in between having a good time.'

And Ed Malcom had laughed and said: 'You don't understand the half of it.'

And Hook had replied: 'But the half I do understand is the half that matters.'

Still and all – a Boosted Man was by his nature in a special position. Even poor old idealistic Ed Malcolm – whose ideas were absolutely right – might not have blinked too hard at the demise of a Novaman.

That is – if he could have known. For, of course, the Boosted Men kept very secret the plans they were working out for the galaxy.

Hook's quick run with the Boosted Man into the shadows out of the actinic-lights of the pedway ended and he dumped the Novir down. In death the Boosted Man took his own personal super-powers with him, and, too, he took the resonance of those powers away from Ryder Hook. He could feel the shimmering change as his body relaxed into an ordinary mortal's half-existence. As always, Hook shuddered with the evil desire to hold on to those dark powers, to let them take over his central core of will, to dominate him as they dominated the Boosted Men.

The Boosted power fell away from Ryder Hook and he was a man once more.

He slid the novir's gun out. It was a Tonota Eighty. That gun seemed to be the workhorse of this sector of the galaxy. No doubt Rafflans had been trying to arrange deals for Krifarm. Business was business in this man's galaxy.

Hook shot the Boosted Man into whiffed nothingness.

That disposed of the corpus delicti; but he couldn't go parading around with a gun in his belt. Hook hated to abandon any weapon. It was against ingrained nature.

He ran swiftly back to the steps of Central Records. He was in slow time now – ordinary time – yet his hundred metre dash would have placed him comfortably in interstellar class in any system. That was thanks to the Powerman Project. During fast-time, of course, his clothes would smoulder and burst into flame unless they were protected, and so he had had to be careful back there when dealing with Welson, as careful as he'd been opening the little ladybird plug in his ear. Now he was a normal man he could look back and whistle at the speed of his reactions then, at the way he'd opened the thing and disconnected the booby-trap and re-circuited the guts of the nasty little enforcer. How he craved Boosted status!

But being fully Boosted all the time brought megalomaniac dreams and desires and an insatiable hunger for more and more power. Being just an ordinary man might be dull; it was safe.

Ryder Hook had never considered himself a safe person though, even when not boosted.

He looked about. In such a decrepit building there were many cracks and crevices. He shoved the Tonota down beside the steps. If a search was carried out here a metal-detector would pick it up at once; he did not think that likely. How many other Boosted Men there might be here in the city he didn't know and how they would explain away the disappearance of the novir he likewise didn't know – and didn't care. By the time they got around to that he intended to be well on the way to doing something drastic about the situation.

But there were other things he must do first, before he started in on these black bastards of Boosted Men.

He walked back slowly yet forcefully towards the hotel.

As he had expected, the man who thought he was a happily-fuddled drunk was dead, thin and exhausted and worn to death, lying abandoned in the gutter.

Chapter Eight

Ryder Hook had never considered himself a very clever man,
although there were those in the galaxy – both human and alien
– who called him the slipperiest bastard in space. Next day on
shift as he looked all about himself and saw the reality of
working conditions, the sights and sounds that would distress
even a tin robot, he knew he was the galaxy's greatest idiot.

For – had he not sent an urgent message to Shaeel, asking the
Hermaphrodite to come to this goddam planet and rescue him?

If Shaeel walked into this little lot . . .

Ryder Hook cursed himself for a fool. Of course, Shaeel was
a monster of perversity, and infuriating, and Hook couldn't
care twopek about ves – but yet, obstinately, he wasn't going to
have the double-barrelled idiot killed. Ve'd come roaring in
from space expecting to pick Hook up from an alienly hostile
environment at the last stages of exhaustion and ve'd pick up
that treacherous homing beacon for the Novamen's local ships
and walk right into it. Shaeel was no Boosted Man, not even a
half a Boosted Man. Shaeel would slave away down here until
ve dropped dead.

That, despite all his rules about self-first, Ryder Hook could
not allow.

So that meant a prime objective must be the spaceport.

The very first target, though, must be information.

Left to his own devices, Hook would simply have blasted his
way into the spaceport, snatched the nearest suitable ship, and
lifted off. This planet of Locus could go hang.

But there was unfinished business, down here . . .

For a start he began to collate information on just what the
Boosted Men were doing down here. They had built an industrial complex that, for all its size, was a ramshackle affair at
best. Its monolithic and imposing aspects had impressed themselves on the workers through this damned hypnotic power.
Now he could see without being subject to false signals being

fed into his brain he could see the towers scattered about the project, latticework constructions with dish radar-like antennae mounted at their summits. From them, surmised Hook, flooded the hypnotic signals.

He saw no further Boosted Men and did not receive any resonances to tell him that a Novaman had passed by.

The orange and blue clad guards and overseers carried out their masters' bidding. Even these people looked drawn and thin and Hook guessed they would not survive the project any better than the workers. The Boosted Men would do what they required and then space out and the installations would rot and the people who were not already dead would die, inevitably.

Off shift he met Anthea outside the tumble-down old apartment block he knew she saw as a luxury hotel.

She wore her bedraggled orange coverall and the chemical and oil stains formed a dismal pattern of servitude across the cheap material. Glimpses of golden flesh gleamed through the rents. For all that, she looked alluringly lovely and desirable; and Hook knew he would have to watch himself far more carefully now she presented a pathetic picture than he had when she was merely a lavishly-gowned and sexy fun-girl of the galaxy. That she had never been did not enter into it. She'd been a simple girl working for her living and out for a holiday with her friend Myza. She was involved in biochemistry, so Hook understood, and he set himself to pry more information from her.

'How do you like my new dress?' she greeted him.

Ryder Hook was not nonplussed.

'Cheeky,' he said, forcing a lightness he did not feel into his words. 'You'll have me leaping on you in the street.'

That hurdled that problem.

By cross-reference with Myza and Rafflans later in the rusty old shed they saw as the first-quality restaurant, he checked out that everyone, including Anthea, thought she was wearing an off-the-shoulder silver-slink gown with scarlet gemstones stitched in the seams. The off-the-shoulder bit was explained by the two massive rips in the orange cloth where she'd evidently caught her coverall on a projecting ledge or sharp-angled piece of machinery. He put a hand on her shoulder. He could feel the silky softness of the golden skin under his own skin – but also he could feel the frightening fleshlessness, the hard angularity of bone underneath.

However maudlin it sounded for tough Ryder Hook, who

couldn't-care-less about other people so long as he was all right, he made up his mind these black bastards of Novamen weren't going to destroy Fraulein Anthea Elterich. He knew that all the workers who had been here when he had arrived would be doomed. They were too far gone. If he could get his party of survivors away they might be saved; he knew he could do nothing for the others. Some subtle radiation, some poison in the inefficiently-filtered air-supply, something tainted this dome and slowly but remorselessly destroyed human life.

And all life was human – be it in the familiar form of Homo sapiens, or the equally familiar form of the alien peoples about them now. Rafflans, a Krifman, was just as human as an Earthman. It was simply that people tended to call themselves human and other races alien.

He wondered about the Reakers, though. Were they fully human as a man would understand it?

Anyway, here they worked as willing tools of the Boosted Men and their overseers. The Reakers must fit into the equation as intelligent life, valuable because of that, but humanity not-proven.

One fact was undeniable.

The Boosted Men were no longer human.

When he and these stranded souls whom he must try to think of as friends solemnly sat in a draughty old barn with sagging doors and collapsing roof and stared hypnotically at a blank wall, he had to join in with the chorus of applause and bravos every now and then as the ghostly, invisible, non-existent orchestra played symphonies and concertos – three whole hours of it.

He excused himself a couple of times, when he thought the moment was propitious, and went outside and looked up at the dome and wondered, and fretted, and went back inside and took up that alert listening pose of complete absorption in phantom music.

Going for a sail aboard a yacht on the lake was nothing short of pathetic.

People in their filthy orange coveralls sat or stood on flat planks of plastic mounted on rubber-tyred universally-swivelled wheels, and trundled around the empty stretch of concrete. A wind was blowing, at least; but Hook found the most profound and strange sensations attacking him as he watched these people laughing and enjoying themselves in this ludicrous and tragic situation.

He was glad to get back into the old shed. They kept on pressing him to drink scummy water from a cracked mug and he kept on trying to drink the nauseous gunk, and eat the slop from the plastic dish, and gagging, until, at last, Anthea said: 'You are sickening for something, Alf? We don't allow disease at all, not where I come from.'

'No. Just out of sorts. Look, Anthea, let's get out of here.'

'You randy old devil,' said Rafflans leering over his mug of scum-water.

'Sure,' said Hook, and then to keep in fashion, added somewhat jerkily: 'You and me both.'

Even Rafflans looked quizzical at that.

Outside under the starlight striking through the dome Hook looked helplessly at Anthea.

If he took the ladybird out of his ear and inserted it in hers so that she could see the reality, he would lapse into the hypnotic illusion spun about them. He'd have to arrange for Anthea to give the ladybird back. That would be cruelty, exquisite cruelty, to her. She would give it back, of that he felt no doubt. But to show her this reality without being able to help her or prevent its recurrence!

No.

He couldn't do that.

Anyway, it would be of more use to open Rafflans' eyes. The big Krifman would be handy in a fight.

Come to that, the idiot Krifman gonil would no doubt at once offer to rip his arms off and wrap them around his neck. That would be Rafflans' style.

Hook's style was far more subtle.

Either that, or far more stupid.

'You look a real mess, Alf!'

Anthea started in on him. She pulled his coverall straight and brushed away at it, not even removing the top surface of oil and chemical stains. The place where a shorting wire had burned a hole – not helped at all by his careful dash in Boosted time – she tut-tutted over and fussed with and, not altering it in the slightest, at last stepped back and said that, well, Alf was reasonably presentable; but only just and at that not in respectable company.

Hook glanced up at the eternally vigilant dishes spewing out their hypnotic commands.

One function of the control exercised over the workers had been made clear. The more you fancied you were in good health and wearing fine clothes, the more other people saw what you expected them to see. That was subtle and cunning and it appealed to Hook. He could understand that kind of neatly precise programming.

Because he knew what he wore and looked like, so some of the effect was cancelled out and Anthea was troubled and saw his smart tunic and trousers as, somehow, not quite smart enough.

But Ryder Hook wasn't fool enough to imagine that by a logical extension of this process he could make the workers see the scene around them in reality.

They were not, after all, Boosted.

He took Anthea off to the ramshackle old apartment block and he made love to her very gently and with tenderness and her own passion kindled in an even more fiery way.

This was the last night he would lie about like a no-good curd, shrinking from the inevitable action he must take.

Tomorrow, as ever was, he'd kick these Boosted Men right where it hurt the most.

On the morrow, as good as his promise, he did not report on shift but took himself along to Central Records.

During the daylight hours robots manned the desk and Hook saw overseers passing in and out checking quotas and rotas and daily orders. The place was a hive of activity.

He was not Boosted . . .

'What do you want here, friend?' demanded the guard at the door.

Hook wasn't sure just what it was he was expected to see. The guard looked mean and hungry, with a gaunt face and a stubble of hair on his chin where his depilatories had either failed him or had run through their allotted time-span of hair-growth suppressant. His hand rested on his gun butt. The gun was a Tonota Forty. He wore a blue crash-helmet and face mask, and he was impatient with the pose he had to take up.

Hook guessed he was supposed to see a fat kindly cop with a gun firmly latched into its holster and almost rusty from disuse.

'Ordered to report here,' said Hook. 'I dunno what it's all about. Electronics bay.'

'Get over to the desk, friend.' The friend stuck in the goon's mouth. 'They'll sort you out.'

'Thanks, officer.'

Still no thrilling tingling of the Boosting effect . . .

Hook walked across to the desk.

The robot said: 'Your business?'

'I've been posted to the Main Building,' said Hook. 'I want fresh clothing and equipment.'

'Door ninety down the hall.'

Hook marched off.

He was said to be utterly ruthless. Well, ruthless he was. He acknowledged that, even as he regretted it. But down here on Locus that ruthlessness had been eroded. He was going to tremendous trouble to save the skins of a group of people who had meant nothing to him before they'd stepped off that shuttle together.

Shaeel – well, ve was somewhat different.

Room ninety offered up robotically-proferred garments. Hook took them, for form's sake, and the tool-kit that came with them. He went out.

Still no Boosting . . .

He went outside and headed for the Main Building.

Here was where all the differing productions of the shops were assembled. Here was where he would find out what it was all about.

The absence of Novamen worried him, though . . .

He had to walk smartly and keep a bright vacuous smile on his face. In the fifty hour day and night cycle of Locus people were exhausted as the shifts wore remorselessly on; but they never fretted or complained. They just went loyally on, smiling away, enjoying themselves, until they fell down dead. Then the Novamen would assign a new body to replace the one carted away. People in the galaxy were always anxious to take good jobs offering high wages, and expected to end up on strange planets. That was all a part of the magic of the whirlpool of stars. This time, though, they'd signed up on a dead end.

He said to the first overseer he met in the foyer of the Main Building: 'I'm assigned here, electronics.'

The overseer looked down his clipboard. He was haggard and yet nowhere as exhausted as the workers. He was a mal, with the tubular ears twisting and turning, and he rolled one of those ears between his fingers and thumb, a gesture characteristic of mals. 'No one told me,' he said.

'Wouldn't you know it,' said Hook. 'It's the same wherever you go in this galaxy.'

The mal looked at him sharply.

No one complained down on Locus.

Hook smiled the wide vacuous smile of the happily hypnotised.

'I'm an electronics man,' he said. He gestured expansively. 'I'll fit in.'

'I suppose it's all IQ. Report to Overman Baynes. I'll check your details out later, Alf.'

'Fine. Let me have my docket back later.'

Hook marched smartly off as though going to work for Overman Baynes was the greatest thing since arch-supports.

He was directed to Overman Baynes by robots and other workers and penetrated into the Main Building. The place was a warren. Hook got the impression these multi-faceted cells concealed and surrounded a massive inner hall. Target priority, then . . .

When Central Records got his docket from the overseer and fed it into central computing they'd come up without a match for electronics-robot-supervisor Alf to report to the Main Building. That might take a long time if the overseer didn't bother to send it across until he came off shift. If he winged it across straight away – oh, well, said Hook to himself as he marched smiling like an idiot up to Baynes, that might not happen. If it did he would be ready.

'Nobody told me,' said Overman Baynes.

Hook smiled. 'I'm here and ready for work, Overman.'

Baynes was big and heavily-built; but he'd lost a lot of fat recently, and his eyes were sunken. He was not Homo sapiens, although very close to that, being Homo siriansis – which had nothing to do with the star Sirius – and only his fleshy crest and the flaps lobed from his ears differentiated him from a sapiens. His hands and arms, built on the usual system rife in the galaxy of a single bone from shoulder to elbow, two bones to give rotation and flexibility, from elbow to wrist, and then a number of smaller bones arranged in a variety of efficient ways according to race, were a trifle on the short side. Apart from tentacles, this skeletal structure was found universally in the galaxy among races who had developed a boney structure and a pair of arms with hands attached. There were other systems; but they were generally less efficient. Nature approximated to a norm even with alien DNA in solving ecological-niche problems.

'And keep up to the quotas,' called Baynes as Hook moved off. 'We're doing highly important work here and if we fall down on it we'll be betraying the econorg.'

'Too true,' said Ryder Hook, loner in the galaxy. 'You can't let your econorg down.'

Directly ahead of him beyond an oval-shaped door of clear crystal which valved as he approached lay a long high-ceilinged chamber. He could see men and women and aliens moving about and every one intent upon their tasks. He checked his work-sheet Baynes had given him. He was to supervise the coupling in of the neural-suppressors. He reached the door and let it hang valved open for a moment.

For that moment he was out of sight of Baynes, who had in any case turned to answer a query from a dishevelled-looking woman carrying a smashed assembly. He looked into the chamber. Down the centre and arranged in a neatly-precise row, stood a line of a hundred tall and narrow boxes. Ryder Hook could estimate beyond guesswork when it came to numbers as low as a hundred, and he knew with a single glance there were exactly a hundred boxes there without the need to count each one.

He knew that intuition which he attempted to deny had brought him to the heart of the problem.

He had to know what he was supposed to see.

But this time he must so programme the command he gave himself that nothing he could forsee could break it.

He stood looking into the room and swiftly detached the ladybird from his ear.

Not instantly; but with bewildering speed, the scene subtly changed focus. The room remained the same, clean and functional. The people now wore smart white clothing, a kind of uniform coverall with shiny buttons which, he discovered on looking down at himself, he also wore. These were the Main Building clothes, then. The boxes showed transparent lids, with pipes running to and from them, pipes which were bundled and colour-taped into outlets in the ceiling. Then his conditioning took over and the ladybird went back with a thud that sounded like an airlock closing on green.

The scene changed again; but Hook saw with intense pleasure that in all important respects it remained the same. Only the people wore clothes that were not at all white or smart. The boxes with their transparent lids, the colour-coded pipes, the banks of instruments. He must be near, now, he must!

He walked on into the chamber and the crystal door at last could valve itself shut.

A woman with a wild mop of yellow hair and eyes of a blue

so startling they must be retinally-dyed, walked up with a smile. She was a dumpy person, a little flabby still, as though she had had plenty of flesh to work on before she came to Locus.

'Hullo,' said Hook, holding out his work sheet.

She glanced down at it.

'I'm Overman Benson and I run this show. I didn't ask for extra help.'

'But I'm sure you could do with an extra pair of hands,' said Hook, pushing that inane smile. This woman could see reality about her, even if she carried a ladybird plug in her ear that controlled her. He had to be careful.

'Have you been checked out?'

'Why, surely. Overman Baynes has it all – '

'All right. Neuro-suppressors. That's Hallipen. Over there.'

She was a sight brisker than anyone he'd met yet. She motioned and still with that smile Hook wandered across. Hallipen was a Fortan, a being whose chief claim to fame lay in the pair of atrophied arms that hung from a small and slender pair of shoulder-blades beneath the shoulder blades of his normal arms. The collar bones ran intricately past his lungs. The arms might be atrophied; but they gave their owner a great advantage in intricate detail work. Hook knew Fortans were fine electronics people.

About to broaden his big stupid smile and hold out his hand, Hook looked into the nearest box. He could see through the transparent lid.

In there, stark naked, laid out, perfect in form and feature, lay the white body of an impossibly beautiful woman.

And Ryder Hook knew.

Chapter Nine

Trust the Boosted Men to pick on a dancing girl of the Shashmeeri!

Hook caught his involuntary hesitation and walked on.

'Sure,' said Hallipen, the Fortan, waving one of his atrophied hands holding a slipstick. 'I fancy her, too; but that's out. Best forget all about that.'

Hook kept his smile going.

'I'm working for the econorg, Hallipen,' he said. 'I know which plug to pull.'

Hook walked on down the line of boxes. Each contained a perfect girl encased within the translucent walls.

Most were Earth girls. But, among the hundred, there were representatives of ten of the alien races reputed to produce the most beautiful females of a terrestial pattern. Mind you, Hook always preferred a real Earth girl. The Shashmeeri were all breast and hip and impossibly so; discretion in amounts of beauty appealed to Hook far more than this carnal obsession with lush profusion. Shape and soft firmness and delicacy, they were the prime-requisites in a woman's breasts; not size.

He picked up the routine of what was going on here. Science could work what appeared to be miracles and if this was bio-engineering on a macro rather than a micro scale, it was none the less for that of intense interest.

What was being done to these perfect examples of female beauty was very similar to what had been done to Hook himself.

They were undergoing treatment that had been pioneered by RCI in their Powerman Project.

The outcome of the final stages of that project, stages from which Hook had been excluded, was the production of Boosted Men.

These girls in their translucent boxes with the transparent lids were being transformed into Boosted Women.

Well, Hook considered, that would be nice for the Novamen.

Without genetic engineering they couldn't hope to breed Boosted boys and girls from these women; but no doubt that would follow all in good time.

Now he could understand the secrecy surrounding Locus.

Hallipen fussed.

'We're almost finished up with this batch, Alf. So you'd best carry out the final check with the neuro-suppressors. I see the work sheet says you were involved in their production.' The Fortan glanced up and – almost but only almost on this happy planet of Locus – a frown appeared on his face. 'It's most unusual for personnel engaged on production of components and bio-tooling to be switched to the end product. Most odd.'

'They must have thought you needed help – '

'Help? Why, we can turn out these young ladies now like peas from a pod! Still, I'll admit I do work hard at it. I can do with some help, at that.'

'There you are, then.'

The information Ryder Hook needed was almost all within his grasp. A few more facts; the last and, given what he already knew, the most vital factor, and then he could see about changing the situation.

Atavistic and vicious though it might be, the idea of doing that gave him some anticipatory pleasure.

The Fortan had to sit down for a spell. He looked ill. Hook said: 'How long have you been here, Hallipen?'

'How long? Oh – now that's odd. I don't seem able to remember clearly. I've to remember the kids' birthdays and they haven't come around, yet – at least, I don't think they have. I hope not.' He stroked his left tiny hand over his chin, whilst his left normal hand propped his head up on his knee. 'How strange that I'm not sure!'

Well, said Ryder Hook to himself, you're another one of the poor devils these bastards of Boosted Men have murdered. Hallipen would never get back to Fortanesi and his kids, that was for sure.

'How long does it take to process a batch of these girls?'

Hallipen tried to stand up, and failed, and subsided. But he went right on smiling.

'You do ask questions! I've never met anyone who asked so many questions. It takes – it takes – '

'All right,' said Hook, growing warm. 'Are any more programmed after this lot?'

Hallipen chuckled. 'Only one. That I know. My contract expires then and I'm off home. I miss the kids.'

Hook turned away.

The strong and gagging odour of chemicals and oil and laboratory wastes circulated in the air. Air conditioning ran at a minimum here. There was no need of refinements of conditions for deluded workers who thought they were having a wonderful time in a good job with hectic pleasures. Men and women and aliens were run at full-speed here, all out, burning up. When they died they could be shovelled out on to the planetary surface and forgotten. They wouldn't be going home.

Hook knew with a sourness he detested and relished that the overseers and the foremen and the Overmen would be discarded, too.

Overman Benson bustled up, her yellow hair seeming to crackle with discharges of static.

'How are you getting along, Alf? We have to keep our quotas up.'

'This batch is prime, Overman. I'm all ready for the next little lot when they arrive.'

'Good. Keep at it. Remember your econorg depends on you!'

There were thousands of rallying-cries for the multi-system conglomerates; passionate exhortations, mottoes, pass-words, secret formulae of words, fine ringing phrases, all designed to make econorg members feel one of a family and to give of their utmost for the mutual good.

Hook didn't spit.

He was supposed to be a stupid hypnotised worker, wasn't he?

This ramshackle city labouring under its encircling web of hypnosis was merely a single tiny spot on the planetary surface of Merfalla, and calling it Locus did not make it any the more important. Outside, the rest of the planet slumbered in indifference, nursing an environment alien and hostile to humans who needed air to breathe and a lack of high-energy radiation. One single city did not make a planet. And this wasn't a real city. For a start there was not one single museum. Hook was a museum nut. He knew that any culture with any pretensions of value, and hope, had to know and understand its own past. The idea of living in the present and the future alone had been tried, plenty of times and in every case – as far as Hook knew – had failed.

Shaeel wouldn't thank him for bringing ves down here.

As Shaeel had said to him once: 'Y'know, 'ook, although my ancestors were produced on Earth I sometimes wonder about you Terrans. I mean – look at all those tridi shows and stories you had about your Terrans going off and conquering the galaxy and smashing up stars along the way – '

'Knock it off!' Hook had said. 'That was kid's stuff.'

'And highly dangerous, you Chancroid Subject for Surgery! How could kids understand about the real galaxy if they're stuffing their fool little heads with maniacal ideas about smashing stars and conquering galaxies and having interstellar wars – intergalactic wars too, my Poor Sainted Aunt Augusta! Don't you fool Terrans know the difference between distances that are interstellar and intergalactic, already?'

Hook had been charmed by that little, tossed in, 'already'.

'We haven't been about conquering anyone for thousands of years – '

'My Sweet Dear Creature 'ook! If I wasn't a Ladylike Gentleman – or a Gentlemanly Lady – I'd kick you in the pants.'

Ve would, too – if ve remembered before some other bright scheme occurred to ves.

Wacky old Shaeel–who could aspirate an 'h' as well as anyone and yet who always insisted on calling Hook 'ook. Shaeel, who had both men and women running after ves. If Hook had the temerity to claim a friend in this galaxy, he might suggest that Shaeel was the nearest he would ever come.

He went across to Overman Benson and leaned down above that electric-crackle yellow hair. He made his smile more meaningful. She looked up, wary and yet preening already.

'You – doing anything after shift, Overman?'

'Why – I had planned; but if you've – '

Hook leaned closer. He was working in ordinary time now. Just why he'd picked on this shrunken-fat little woman wasn't perfectly clear, except that he had to start somewhere. After all, he supposed she wasn't entirely to blame, for just how the Boosted Men selected their Overmen and other grades of overseers remained a mystery. He reached up, smiling into her eyes, conscious that his own brown eyes looked clear and frank and shining with integrity, and tweaked her left ear.

'Really, Alf! I like a little nudge and wink – but Hallipen is – '

He performed the operation smoothly, a twisting dive in and out. Overman Benson gave no indication that she had noticed anything. Still smiling at her, Hook palmed the ladybird plug and stepped back.

'You're all IQ, Overman.'

She glanced around, puzzled. The chamber had not altered a great deal for her; but Hook knew that to her eyes he had suddenly put on a dazzlingly-white coverall with shiny buttons. She shook her head. Hook felt no sympathy. She was dead, anyway, as soon as the Boosted Men finished here. And getting her off-planet at once still would not save her. The bodily rot induced by conditions here had gone too far. To save Anthea – and Rafflans and Myza and Denis and the other passenger survivors from *Talcahhuano* – must be the first priority if there was any rescuing to be done.

He took himself off to the washroom. The tools in the kit supplied were adequate although they were not of the superbly high quality of his own tools in his boots. He had to take a damned sight more care opening the bug this time and de-activating the booby-trap. He was in ordinary time, now; he was skilled and a master electronics operator and yet he had to sweat this one out where before, in speed-time, he'd gone in with the superhuman touch of a Boosted Man.

There lay the danger, of course – the insidious craving for power one always said one would resist. The knowledge that difficult tasks were made easy. The sheer power over circumstances and events. By Dear Old Dirtie Berti Bashti! No wonder the Novamen clung to their Boosted status!

He went back into the chamber and through the oval crystal door.

He did not even consider giving the ladybird to Hallipen. The Fortan was a scientist, and had enough training to understand that the sickness within him was terminal in scope. Disease, sickness, these were the obscenities of the galaxy now, used as swear-words, loathed, feared when outbreaks such as the pandemic that had caused all the trouble back on Mcrgone broke out against all normal sanity. Disease had been conquered – the kind of conquest that meant something when set against insane kiddy-nonsense of conquering galaxies – and yet the foulness persisted in striking back at humanity in new and hideous Medusa guises.

He took Overman Baynes's ladybird with a simple sleight-of hand trick, an adaption of one of the many card-sharp tricks he whiled-away boring hours practising when forced to do so, and de-bugged it. With the two ladybirds he went to find Anthea and Rafflans.

In the foyer of the Main Building the overseer Hook had first spoken to here looked up and called: 'Hey! Alf! There's a coupla guys looking for you. Lucky you walked by.'

In the first goon's hand the docket Hook had passed over indicated clearly, without doubt, that he had been rumbled.

The enforcer wore a mean look that, Hook supposed, he would see as a paternal frown, a concerned consideration for his own welfare. Both goons had the flaps of their holsters un-zipped and the gun-butts shone dully under the lights. Both were men, one a Homo sapiens the other a Homo mal, and they were both tough, big-chested, mean and ready to blast him down the instant he gave them trouble.

But, first, they would have to play it with sweetness and light, according to the dictates of the Boosted Men who kept their workers happy.

'Alf? Oh – there's a little problem come up – nothing serious. We'll just go along to Central Records and sort it all out.'

He was perfectly at their disposal and happy to go with them, although he couldn't for the life of him understand what there could be wrong. And he had a schedule to keep – the neuro-suppressors had –

'Sure, sure,' said the first goon. 'But this won't take long.'

'No time at all,' affirmed the second goon, the mal, affably. He chuckled, a fat happy cop making a silly little chore into a joke. 'You know these office types and their dockets.'

'There's nothing to worry about,' said the first goon. 'Down here on Locus we're all one big happy family.'

'Sure, that's right,' said the second enforcer. 'You just come along with us, Hook.'

Chapter Ten

Ryder Hook was not fool enough to imagine the mal would miss the slip. Even if he did, the man wouldn't.

To Ryder Hook, in that moment, the feeling of a great weight slipping off his shoulders gave him the sense of expanding his lungs and of breathing a huge draught of fresh air. He was free.

He hit the man in the guts and the mal in one tubular ear. Then he ran outside.

He was in ordinary time; but he felt wonderful, all the same.

Exactly how much information the Boosted Men here had assembled into his dossier he had no way of knowing. Certainly, RCI had a file on him. The Novamen would not be able to lay their hands on his records with EAS through any ordinary channels, and, anyway, no one – apart from the department – knew that Ryder Hook had once been Jack Kinch. Other econorgs and solar system governments kept files on him. They might be assembled into a package that would give enough of a run down to alert and worry the Novamen. Hook had had to fight in the dark before.

This time, he felt convinced that he was being sought because the forensic men on Locus had matched up his traces with those found about the pilot's throne of the shuttle. They wanted him for smashing up their spaceship. They'd taken a long time to catch up with him; but they'd got there in the end.

That poxed docket had done it, of course.

Regrets were not in Ryder Hook's style.

He hared off down the street.

If he was fool enough to allow himself to be taken in, and questioned, the sophisticated computer equipment the Novamen would have here would rapidly – very rapidly – tie him in with this Ryder Hook who caused so much trouble. He had to assume that. There was no time to spare at the moment to cut into whatever apparet net might be operating here and find out. Hook would take the situation at its worst and plan on that, and if the scene wasn't really as bad as that, why, then he was laughing.

Not that he laughed much.

He'd probably laughed more down on Locus recently than he had in the last year.

He ran on and laughed gleefully when orange-clad work people looked at him, made signs, motioned to them to join him. He was just a happy drunk of Locus, out on a spree.

He'd like to see Locus burned up.

The poor dupes inhabiting the tragically funny city would suffer anyway. He had to keep thinking that. Ruthless, tough, uncaring Ryder Hook – he had to keep reminding himself these people were already doomed.

He found Myza taking a break in a small bar opposite the factory. She giggled when he panted up.

'Fancy your chances, Alf?'

'Where's Anthea?'

'Working, of course. Our shifts were changed – have a drink.'

The scummy mess in a cracked tin cup might be foul coffee or wine or lager, for all he knew.

'Not right now, thanks, Myza.'

He started across the street towards the factory gates and Myza called: 'You won't find Anthea there, Alf.'

He swung about. His face puzzled Myza. Hypnotised into seeing bland smiles all the time she couldn't really comprehend the filthy black rage spreading on Hook's face.

'She's been transferred – I told you we'd changed shifts.'

'Yes, you told me that, you stup – you told me. But where's Anthea?'

'She's filling in at the Main Building. Something about a hitch in production there. But Anthea's bio-medical you know.'

'Yes, I know.'

He daren't trust silly empty-headed Myza with the ladybird. If he gave it to her to pass on to Anthea and told her to tell Anthea to put it in her left ear, Myza would be sure to do that herself, first. Then – no, it wasn't worth the furore.

'Never mind, Myza.' Her frown annoyed him. 'I'll see you tonight.' If it was a lie nothing showed. 'Cheerio.'

'I always said you were an odd one, Alf.'

He walked away holding down the screaming urgency that told him to run, run!

He'd find Rafflans at the weapons shop, for sure. Their shifts coincided. If the big Krifman tried to rip his arms off and wrap them around his neck he'd hit Rafflans, so help him, he would!

Why in all the stars of the galaxy had Anthea been shifted into the Main Building now?

He'd have to go and find her, of course; but he had to get the order in which he did all the things he had to do right. Anthea would have to wait.

Still wearing the white Main Building overalls with their shiny buttons he nipped around the back of the bar building. As he had expected a couple were sitting on an upturned heap of rubbish – God knew what they thought they were sitting on – drinking goo from battered plastic cups. The young man was of a sufficiently broad-shouldered build to suit. The girl looked exhausted with sagging dark smudges beneath her eyes and a tremble all along her limbs. The two were in the middle of the preliminaries, and Hook felt a stirring of some emotion or other in his flinty heart. Which was a nice romantic way of putting it.

He walked up behind them, knuckled them both gently under the ears and caught them, one in each arm as they fell.

The lad's coverall fitted well enough and Hook pulled and wriggled the worst rips into shape. Then he looked at the girl. She did not only look pathetic, lying there with the near-translucent lids of her eyes closed above those brutal blue bruises, she was pathetic.

Hook took off her coverall too, and looked without change of expression on the way her ribcage protruded, the flabbiness of her young breasts, the thinness of her waist. He draped the naked girl and boy neatly together, hands so, lips touching, and stood back and took not a whit of humour from it. Let them get what love they could while they still lived.

He hoped they'd have the sense to get on with it when they woke up from where he'd left them off.

A patrol flier went howling down the street, five metres off the pavement, and people turned to look and wave. Hook waved right along with the other zombies.

Just how the Boosted Men running this show would break the news to their dupes that a dangerous man was loose among them had intrigued Hook. If everything down here on Locus was so hunky-dory, how come anyone could be dangerous? Or loose? That meant there were other people here who weren't loose.

But they were Boosted Men and they'd flick into speed time and figure a way.

Hook glanced up the metalloy skeleton mast with its dish aerial focused on this area. If there were spy eyes up there they'd know he was here. If there were not, they wouldn't. The matter did not admit of argument.

Hook shinned up the latticework. Had Shaeel been able to see him now, for all the suns in space ve'd say something like: 'You great hairy Terran-spiderman, 'ook!'

Shaeel could be very cutting at times.

Perched on the top cross bar, Hook dug down into his boot again. He produced a tiny power-loop. This was just about the most simple and effective way of discovering just where energy was flowing. It didn't tell him what kind, though; just at the moment Hook felt he already had that information.

He held the loop angled and swung it in sweeps before the aerial dish. The air was filled with energy. Beamed energy, of course, had its drawbacks; the chief obstacle to successful use of beamed power which would do away with pylons and power lines had been the sheer enormousness of the power, the frying-power of the energy. Nowadays there was no danger in Hook perching himself in the path of mega-amps to the nth power.

The loop tingled and indicated a direction. Hook stared that way. Certainly, a building which might be a power station bulked over there, hidden beyond trees. They were real trees for he could see them and he was not hypnotised. A dome flashed in the sunlight striking through the outer dome above. That might be the place. He'd need a cross-fix to make sure.

'Hey! You up there! You'll injure yourself!'

Hook looked down.

A guard had walked out from beyond the bar and, just for the moment, was hidden by the rubbish heap from the two naked potential lovers. Hook stowed the loop and waved.

'Lovely day, officer! Admiring the view.'

He shinnied down halfway.

He squinted down past his legs. The guard had unlimbered his gun. It was a Tonota Forty. So the guard was not a fool, then.

At least, not a complete fool. He must guess this was the man Hook they were supposed to be looking for and no doubt had already called that information out to his headquarters. He had the sense to draw his gun. He didn't have the sense to steer well clear of Ryder Hook.

Hook pushed and sprang and fell on top of the guard. He had no need to hit him. Hook stood up and pulled his coverall straight. The guard lay folded up, like a badly-made sausage. Hook took his gun and transceiver but didn't stay around to swap uniforms.

He took off along the street, diagonally across the pedway, aiming for a right-angled fix on the possible power station. He slowed to a walk and looked idiotically cheerful when a flier went past. They'd have ident kits issued soon, and then he might have more difficulty in avoiding observation.

The gun and transceiver he'd stowed in his tool kit. That looked authentic, a sight common on a million planets.

When he reached a pylon supporting a dish that he figured would be near-enough a right-angle – that was in a sense a council of perfection as he had no intention of using a three-way fix – he climbed up. If speed was a weapon it had always been cracked up to be, then speed was necessary now.

He swung the loop, aligning it between the dish and the distant gleam of the power-station dome. The loop refused to tingle. Hook cursed. He swung it about and when he felt the tingle, sighted, and admitted that he did feel surprise.

Between the power station and the first dish he had looped of its telenergy lay a single park-like expanse unique in the city under its dome. The loop tingled exactly on line with the centre of the park.

All Hook could see there was a clump of trees – and he didn't even know their names, let alone what planet they had been brought from.

He climbed down fast and belted across the pedway and into a side-alley between a refrigerated store and an apartment house.

Two guards paced across the mouth of the alley and Hook froze. When they had gone he relaxed. At first he had wondered why, with this magical hypnosis going for them, the Boosted Men bothered with guards. One reason was obvious. People all over the galaxy were accustomed to having their social life looked after and guarded by police. One econorg looked after its own, and goons and enforcers made sure their econorg wasn't pushed around. So the stalemate existed, in which peace was the norm. Had there been no guards here the people might have complained.

And no one ever complained about lily-white Locus.

The other reason lay in a vague rumour Hook had picked up in a bar – a real, brawling, disgusting spaceman's bar – out past the Rockington Cluster – a bunch of hard-cases out there – which a one-eyed wart had told him in a confidential whisper in between the strips. There was a bunch operating in the galaxy who didn't give a damn for econorgs. At first Hook had thought the little guy had in some way caught a whisper of the Boosted Men. But it wasn't like that. The wart mentioned a name – Untergods – then looked over his shoulder and clammed up. But if such a group did exist and the Boosted Men knew of them; maybe they posed threat enough for this secret project to be guarded as it was.

Having not nearly settled where the hypnosis signals were being beamed from, Hook, disgruntled enough to rip Rafflans' fool Krifman arms and legs off first, trundled off to find the Krifarm expert.

The weapon shops were guarded, of course, and Hook prowled. Had the guards not been there he wouldn't have gone within a kilometre of the place, and Rafflans could have gone hang. As it was he took a guard between his fingers, dropped him senseless on the stones, slid his knuckles behind the ear of the fellow's comrade and then walked boldly, smiling all over his face, through the entrance way.

He would have very little time inside.

The ident kits would be issued by now – had he been running security he'd have been toppling heads if they weren't – and they'd be programmed to sniff, scent and detect him by means of matches with what the computer said were Ryder Hook's bodily secretions . . .

Men and women worked here in much the same way they worked in the electronics bay. Robots were everywhere. Hook pushed through, smiling, carrying a snatched-up box full of components. He didn't bother with the lower echelons. If Rafflans was all he said he was, he'd have been put in charge of something important. Hook found the Krifman poring over the three-dimension illuminated cube of a blueprint. The old name was still used. Rafflans looked up.

'Why, hullo, Alf! Great to see you!'

Hook lowered the unconscious body of Rafflans' woman assistant to the floor. He slid the door of the little cubby-hole office shut. Rafflans gaped.

'What – what happened to Queenie?'

'Rafflans, you great Krifman twit! Put this in your ear.'

Rafflans objected; but Hook grabbed him by the neck, twisted his head, smacked the ladybird in.

Hook stepped back.

Rafflans shook his head. He reached up – and then he looked at the crumpled form of Queenie in her threadbare orange coverall, smothered in gun-grease and chemicals, ripped down one leg, disgusting, like them all. Rafflans choked.

'Queenie! What in hell's going on! Alf – no, *Hook*!'

'Yes. Hook. And when you look around you, just keep that great idiotic Krifman grin on your ugly puss.' Hook spoke fast. He spoke with a controlled fury that sobered the Krifman. He explained all he considered necessary. Rafflans said: 'I was going to rip – '

Hook said: 'Later. I've got to go to the spaceport. Here's a ladybird for Anthea. If you take one from an overseer or a guard and try to open it you'll blow your fingers off.'

'You forget, Hook. I'm a weapons expert.'

'So all right, then. It's a dinky little twist on the Marden-reef trembler – five stages – each one lethal.'

Rafflans nodded. 'I know it. I can defuse that junk.'

'Don't say I didn't warn you. The circuit to rip is easy to spot.' Hook checked the Krifman out, and added: 'There may not be time. This place is scheduled to fall to pieces soon. They've got one more batch of women to process.' He had told Rafflans that they were programming women for a purpose far different from Boosting. The fight between him and the Boosted Men was one for him, and if anyone, including a bunch of mythical Untergods got in the way he'd shoo them off, too.

'I'll sort out a few heavies, Hook. Are you coming back from the spaceport?'

Hook knew what the Krifman meant.

'Yes. We'll get away together, all of us. And there's another little chore I have unfinished here – '

A siren began to wail.

'That's you, Hook.'

'Right. Remember to carry on acting like an idiot.' Hook stepped over Queenie, who was groaning and beginning to come around. 'That should be dead easy, you stupid great Krifman twit.'

'Sure, you black bastard of an Earthman. All I need do is copy you.'

Hook ran out feeling much better.

Chapter Eleven

Ryder Hook could count on the unpredictability of Shaeel.

The transceiver he had taken from the guard was useless. He might fix it to operate within this solar system; it just wouldn't carry into interstellar space. He went hunting for a set that would do what he wanted.

He had the advantage in this hide and seek that he looked just like any other hypnotised worker on the street and the sniffer ident kit detectors needed a little time to gather sufficient data on which to come up with a positive.

If he kept on the move and didn't do anything stupid he could avoid capture at least until he'd rigged a set and reached Shaeel.

He went down to the flier park and knocked out a couple of guards. They both wore Tonota Forties and he took them both. The flier he selected had been locked; but he jimmied the panel with a sweet little tool from his boot and climbed in. He took off and drove dangerously low and fast towards the airlocks. He had chosen the guards' own flier, of course, and when the guard on the airlocks came on he half-turned his face away from the screen and snarled in a vicious tone: 'Open up, you morons! Don't you know there's an emergency on?'

The airlocks valved.

He went through with scarcely a pause between opening and closing and if anyone had the temerity to accost him he guessed they thought better of it. He knew only too well the way Boosted Men treated their underlings.

For whatever reason the spaceport had been sited away from the city dome, it was inconvenient for him; but he had to be on hand in case – that was the way Ryder Hook played the odds – and he'd combine that greeting with the use of an interstellar set.

Getting into the spaceport was so easy he knew at once he had been discovered,

The locks valved for him and he dived into reception.

That short trip across the planetary surface had revealed dun brown grass-like vegetation, a river or two – they were possibly water rivers – and scraggly trees and dispirited mountains. No doubt the poles were iced up and the equatorial regions a little more lavish with flora. Reception looked like any other reception area; smooth floor, kiosks, booths, counters for business transactions, a rest area. The flier skated through glass doors, smashed a vending machine booth into fragments. Smoke puffed. People were running and screaming in all directions.

The flier cascaded in a showering smother of glass panes and veneered plastic and scraps of once-useful machinery onward through the far wall and came to rest in the locker rooms. Dust drifted down and already flames were eating away the plastic partitions.

Hook stepped from the wrecked flier with something like an evil grin plastered all over his face. He'd enjoyed that. It wasn't often he had the privilege of bringing a flier slap bang into reception.

He went out past the hole in the far wall where the flier's nose had drilled through the plastic colour-sheeting.

He stood on the concrete of a bay where loading robots went about their work with methodical care. A human supervisor was standing staring at the wall, through which protruded the nose of the flier, like a man who sees a devil stick his head through the tridi screen.

Hook bounced over to him, said: 'Happy dreams,' and hit him. He went on, walking jauntily, well aware that he would not have felt like this had he been forced against his will to hit an innocent bystander. Those days had passed; although they might easily return.

Around the corner of the reception building where already a few lazy flames were licking up to be extinguished at once and most effectively by the sprinkler systems, he spotted what he felt might be interesting.

A robot team with a fire appliance had speeded up and were now busily unreeling in readiness to go in to support the automatics. The fire chief was a Homo sapiens. That was a break. The loading robot supervisor, although human, had been a tensor, and they were built like broomsticks, with shoulders so narrow that Hook had not a hope in hell of donning the tensor supervisor's uniform.

He ran past the fire robots with their equipment. He leaped

on to the fire truck which hung a metre off the ground, shouting: 'Hurry 'em up! The automatics are overloaded.'

The man began to utter some blasphemy or other; but Hook knuckled him, not particularly gently, and his fingers were ripping the zips open before the man started to collapse.

Hook flung the uniform on. It was a smart blue, with black belt, and his own boots fitted admirably. He stuffed the limp body of the man into his borrowed orange coveralls, and bundled him under the firetruck. The antigrav field would not harm him. Then Hook, feeling that so far he had kept one step ahead of the reception committee, sprinted for the control tower.

The control tower reached up and connected at its centre point with the dome surrounding the spaceport. Four valves arranged like leaves on a tree segmented the dome down the four compass cardinal points. He slowed to a walk and went in the ground floor entranceway, where robots, men, aliens and Reakers – among others he didn't bother to categorise – were milling.

And, still, there was no thrilling sensation of being Boosted . . .

That might let him down, goddammit to hell!

He watched the confusion for a moment. Ryder Hook claimed he was a man who liked to play safe, and only take a chance when he was pretty sure it wasn't a real chance, when he was sure he would have things his own way. It began to look as though he'd seriously miscalculated the odds this time.

If a Boosted Man didn't show up soon, he'd be done for.

He'd felt absolutely convinced a Boosted Man would be at the spaceport. It had seemed to him one place where the Novamen would wish to keep an eye on operations.

He fretted, and walked about looking important, and occasionally shouted an intemperate order to a gang of robots or Reakers.

At that, it felt great to be back in the old familiar badtempered, insulting, intolerant galaxy again.

He worked his way up the storeys and on the way changed his clothes yet again, this time into the blue uniform of a traffic controller. The poor man had climbed downstairs because the gravshafts were filled with men hunting for this character Hook, and Hook left him unconscious and stripped in a stall in the lady's washroom. Not that that would worry a modern miss of the galaxy. But it relieved the tedium.

And then, as he went through a plastic door marked: 'Communications, off-limits to non-authorised personnel,' he felt the jingling tingling ringling up his spine and down his arms and legs, and knew a Boosted Man had at last come within range of the resonances their bodies mutually set-up. He knew that a Boosted Man, being Boosted all the time even if he did not employ his boosted powers at all times, did not pick up this exchange, that the resonances which now flowed and pulsed through Hook's body flowed and pulsed through a Boosted Man's body all the time.

Lucky devil!

He felt great.

He went into speed-time at once. The people around him stood or sat in frozen stasis, barely moving in real time.

Inside the communications set-up he could select the set he wished to use; but once he began to use it he must of necessity drop down into real time. So – he selected the set farthest away from the shift section leader. He pulled the blue shirt and slacks off the operator, pulled off his own traffic control uniform, put on the shirt and slacks.

He had to work carefully within speed parameters so as not to set the clothes alight as he whipped the operator outside and propped him in the gents. Back inside he stuffed the traffic control uniform under the set with the ladybird bug he had taken from the operator. The booby trap and information channel circuit had come out so fast that he cursed as he remembered his careful handling of the deadly booby trap when he'd been in slow time.

He shot a look around the wide room with its fluoros and its various sets, now all caught as it were in the act of communicating with the galaxy. Those sets must serve a Boosted Men network. Well, there were a lot of them, and that meant the Boosted Men were expanding among the stars.

Here and now he had to concentrate on one thing at a time.

The set was a simple affair, standard communications equipment. He set the controls, flopped down in the seat in the professional communications' man's crouch, and switched back to ordinary time. At once the room came alive with the muted hum and flicker of electrics, of men channelling messages out to the far stars.

Keeping his voice low, and his body blocking off the screen from the next operator, Hook said: 'HGL agency, Lancing.'

Any communications man with the necessary skill could patch himself in across the lightyears, from centre to centre he could make as many free calls throughout the galaxy as he wished. Time lags on the ftl communications systems multiplied, of course, and eventually a message would coagulate and a repeat would have to be flashed to get it further on over the parsecs. But this little set, alone, could take his voice and face out better than a hundred parsecs.

'HGL Lancing.'

'Records.'

'HGL Lancing. Records.'

'What flight did Taynor Shaeel take?' He checked his memory back and gave the local date and time he wanted.

'HGL Agency Lancing. Taynor Shaeel hired starpacket *Watchling* and left Lancing. Destination Mergone.'

Trust Shaeel to do it in style. No starship line for ves. Ve'd hired a small fast starship all ves own. And, also, Mergone was a neat place to give as your flight plan destination if you were really going to Merfalla. Hook felt an unease he knew to be alarm.

He'd brought Shaeel into this mess, and the Hermaphrodite was on ves way and all ready to carry out the great space rescue.

But there was a puzzling time lag, a discrepancy Hook could only explain by Shaeel's notorious unpredictability. The operator at the next set along was giving Hook a puzzled glance and it was leaving time again.

Hook cursed.

He twiddled his dials and punched the sequence that ought to connect him with traffic. If it didn't he had at most a minute left before the adjacent operator leaned across with a query.

Traffic came up. Breathed deeply.

'Traffic records.'

'Traffic records.'

'Log of arrivals – ' Hook held his tongue fast, and let the request go through as that. If he pinpointed what he was looking for the tape record down in Records would unfailingly lead the forensic boys to their quarry. His call to Lancing had been unregistered.

The log began to unreel on the screen.

Hook felt no shock at the numbers of ships involved.

The Boosted Men had an operation of some size going here on Locus. It was an evil operation, Locus was evil; but for now he had to pick out the arrival he did not wish to find.

He let out a sigh.

The log entry was simple: 'Starpacket *Watchling*, inbound

from Lancing.' Then, added in a different mechanical script: 'Special detail.'

Hook kept his emotions under control.

He switched to fast time, shucked off the shirt and slacks, whipped out and brought the frozen form of the operator back, dressed him, propped him in his chair. He collected the traffic control uniform, donned it, checked the ladybird was still there, and whistled out of communications. Let the adjacent operator lean across now, and he'd find his suspicions confirmed. His oppo was sick, no doubt about it.

And all the time the screaming accusation of guilt flamed in Hook's mind.

He felt lacerated.

These black bastards of Boosted Men had taken Shaeel.

Nothing else could have happened.

If the Boosted Man who was giving Hook his fantastic powers should have appeared then, Hook would have shot the bastard's guts out through his backbone, slapbang, and to eternal hell with all the fine notions people like Ed Malcom cherished.

He calmed down.

NO – he wouldn't do that. He needed his Boosted powers now more than he had ever done before.

A spot of the old question and answer session was needed now. That 'special detail' entry meant what it said. Shaeel had been taken off the starpacket and if ve hadn't been killed out of hand ve'd been interrogated on ves reasons for coming to Merfalla. When ve'd successfully hoodwinked them – as Hook knew the Hermaphrodite could do if they didn't go too deep – ve'd be packed off to the city to work.

The thought of work and Shaeel in conjunction, even in that dismal situation, had Hook's thin lips quivering.

Shaeel and work were sworn enemies.

Moving in speed time burned up the calories, and Hook knew he'd be raging hungry soon. But he had things to do before he could think about eating.

Hook went roaring out and down the stairs so fast that the traffic control uniform began to char and then burst into flames.

With a curse that would have consumed what the flames missed he ripped the uniform off and disposed of it down a disposall. Naked but for his boots, those famous old black boots that wouldn't burn if you stuck them in a furnace, he raced down into the basement. The grav shafts were full of goons looking for him and, anyway, they'd have been too slow.

In the basement he found a set-up which, familiar as it was, sickened him afresh. They had a series of barred cells, and they had a discipline cell. He whistled through all of them, looking in but not going into the discipline cell. He saw a number of people, mostly goons undergoing punishment; but no sign of Shaeel. He made his breathing steady and even. He selected the toughest, meanest, nastiest specimen of prison guard and came up behind him, took his neck in his left hand, squeezing, and dragged the guy back into the shadows.

He switched back to slow time.

He smacked the goon around the head.

'Listen, gonil, and listen good!'

The man – he was a Homo sapiens – started struggling, quite unable to comprehend how he suddenly found himself in a dark corner with a madman draped around him, hitting him.

Hook hit him again and said: 'I want straight answers, or else – ' And he levered down. The goon yelled and Hook's right palm came across and caught the scream.

'A Hermaphrodite was brought down here. Special detail. Tell me where ve is, and fast.'

Letting off the pressure on the man's jaw bones, Hook let him speak. The words came out full of bravado, tough, bitter, vicious.

'I know who you are! You're Hook – the maniac. Well, I won't tell you any – '

Hook was somewhat unkind to him.

After a moment, the guard said: 'It was taken to the hospital – '

Hook hit him again, said: 'A Hermaphrodite is not an "it", curd, a Hermaphrodite is a "ve". Remember, next time.' Then Hook put the guy to sleep.

Out of the ghastly prison and punishment basement, follow green arrows, haring down the corridors, racing and running at top speed in speed time – on and into the hospital. Race down the beds in the wards, a few superficial scratches, a broken leg or two, no disease, of course, all industrial injuries, down to the far end, through the crystal door that had no time to valve itself open but was shot into shining shards by the Tonota Forty, on and into the special ward – and there was Shaeel.

Shaeel!

The room was small, with a suspended bed, a table, a call-out box, and another bed dragged out from the wall and at right angles to the first. Hook saw Shaeel in the suspended bed. He

86

saw the squat and unlovely body of a F'lovett in the other bed lying with both massive arms clamped to the bed rails. He looked again at Shaeel, and he stopped and switched back to real time, and laughed.

Shaeel looked up.

'There you are, 'ook. Hand me that nappy, will you, the little blighter's burping all over me.'

One of Shaeel's breasts was exposed from the pyjama suit ve wore. That breast was fuller and rounder than ever Hook had noticed it before, and Shaeel's breasts had been long a bone of contention between them. Hanging on to that full and shining breast, sucking away for dear life, a baby Hermaphrodite glugged and gurgled and burped.

'You old devil!' said Hook. 'You're a mother!'

'And a father too, 'ook, although not to the same child. Now don't be tiresome, 'ook, my dear chap. Hand me the nappy.'

Chapter Twelve

'So that's what delayed you. You were having a baby!'

'I was pregnant at the time, 'ook, that I'll admit. If you understood half of what motherhood meant, You Great Hairy Masculine – '

'Do you know the father?'

'Of course. I've always been fond of Thalleyr – ve's a great maph.' Maph was what Hermaphrodites called themselves. 'And I decided it was time I began a family. You know how it is in the galaxy, 'ook.'

'Yes, I know. But you chose a lulu of a time. Who's this?'

'May I present Karg. He has been invaluable. Karg, this is – '

'Check,' said the F'lovett in a hoarse and gravelly voice like a caisson grinding up a causeway. 'Ryder Hook. This mother-hood-doped idjit talks of nothing else.'

'I'll Deal With You for that Foul Calumny,' said Shaeel. Ve pulled the baby free with a cluck of pure enjoyment, began to feed the insatiable monster on the other side. 'Thing is, 'ook, my old Berti Bashti. Why are we here and why are you not wearing your clothes?'

Hook could not tell Shaeel of the Boosted Men.

'Thing is, Shaeel, you maniac, we have to get out of here. All four of us.'

'I'll grant you that. Most Uncouth, these fellers.'

'First thing, stick this in your ear.' Hook handed across the ladybird. He looked at Karg the F'lovett. The alien was short, chunky, square and very very powerful. His thick arms could crush in a beer barrel. His face, something like the face one might expect to find on a Homo sapiens, was characterised by an extreme ferocity of expression, which was normal, and which changed to an expression of docile imbecility when the F'lovett became annoyed.

Karg looked very happy and contented.

That meant he was a raging fury all ready to boil over.

Hook lifted the ladybird out of his ear and held it. He was programmed to thrust it back if anything changed – but the hospital cell remained exactly as it was. He handed the ladybird to Karg. 'If you take that out of your ear, you're done for. Now,' he began to work on the metalloy linked bonds holding Karg's massive arms down. 'You play it along as well as you can and get the starpacket ready. I've some people to bring out of a city back there. Be ready to go.'

'There are a lot of fellows up there who don't like us,' said Karg very mildly and sweetly. That meant he'd break their backs if he got them in his grasp.

'I know. How you hold the gate open is up to you.' Hook glanced at Shaeel who was serving high quality milk. 'Motherhood softens the brain, so I've heard.'

'Ah, but, 'ook, my Great Hairy Cretinous Friend. Motherhood and Fatherhood in the one person – you can't ante-up on that.'

'When I play cards with you, Shaeel, is when I've rigged the deck so even you can't spot a ringer from a grounder.'

'Don't happen, my dear friend 'ook, to have a pack or deck of cards with you now?' Then Shaeel recognised Hook's state of nakedness and ve shook ves head. 'No. That, I think, is beyond even you.'

'Don't bank on it.'

Shaeel's shoulders and arms were smooth and yet strong, like a man's; ves waist was in normal circumstances small and ves hips flared proudly like a woman's. Ve was neither clearly a man nor clearly a woman. Ves face resembled an ancient – a very ancient – Greek statue, bereft of overt sexual symbols, smooth and beautiful and somehow heart-rending. As for this motherhood bit; Hook felt outraged that Shaeel's beautiful breasts should be so gorged and swollen and fat. Ves hair, a delightful tint of auburn, hung tumbled about ves gleaming golden shoulders. As for the baby, it would grow up to be a maph, neither man nor woman, and no doubt would be as infuriating as its mother.

Hook knew, too, that during this special time Shaeel's masculine organs of reproduction would tend to diminish in size, situated as they were just above his female organs. By the time the baby was weaned, Shaeel would have both sets back to normal. Although he had not so far witnessed the act, it was said that Hermaphrodites enjoyed more sheer fun than single-sexed people; this Thalleyr, whom Hook had met, would also around this time be giving birth to a child who would be in a very special way twin to the one just produced by Shaeel.

It was all very gentle and civilised and by arrangement.

But what a time to choose!

'Karg, you'll have to get ves and the child out.'

Karg stretched his massive arms and grunted and stood up. He reached to Hook's stomach. But he overlapped on both sides.

'I'll look after the f'fafling, Hook. All IQ.'

'I'm not your f'fafling, Karg, and Don't You Forget It!' yelped Shaeel. Then ve winced and yanked and the baby's mouth went plop. 'A tooth already, so help me!'

Hook gave them the three Tonota Forties.

'Keep them thinking they're in charge until the last minute. I'm off now, back to the city.'

'How long do we wait?' Karg spoke ferociously, which meant he was being casual.

'Give me until an hour after dark.' Hook looked at them, at Shaeel with ves baby, and Karg with his chunky powerhouse of a body. 'No more. Check?'

'We'll wait, Hook – '

'Your Return Will Be Keenly Anticipated, 'ook – '

Hook went outside the hospital prison cell and, just before he switched into speed time he leaned against the wall. He had to chuckle. Here he'd called out to Shaeel for help, and the maph had come roaring in, pregnant or no, and landed in this mess. Trust Shaeel to introduce the note of the absurd. But – and here Hook stood up and lost his chuckle – Shaeel had not been on form. He'd noticed ves attempts to rally, to be ves old self. But Shaeel had gone through a rotten experience, bringing another life into the galaxy in prison.

Worry over Shaeel had affected Hook, too. Whilst he was in the Boosted state the hypnosis did not affect him, so there had been no need for his little pantomime of a programme. Had the cell been any different, Shaeel and Karg would have told him.

Then he shifted to fast time.

Hermaphrodites had been the direct result of a space programme initiated back on Old Earth. That had been during a period of galactic expansion when the desire to cram as many people as possible into a starship had been superseded by the idea of sending as few as possible but of giving them double the chances of reproduction. Instead of having to provide two people – a man and a woman – in order to produce offspring; the idea had seemed perfectly valid that each person should be able to perform both halves of the equation. Sperm banks were fine for an all-woman crew. Incubators were fine for an all male crew. But where was the fun and the sound basis for a future life-style in that?

So science had performed once again, and two sets of equipment externally and all the necessary interior plumbing had been installed, as Shaeel would put it when ve was a little high on rum, on which ve doted. The plan had worked for a time; then a whole new cataclysm had swept over Old Earth, and the plan had been abandoned. But the result was that there was in the galaxy a happy and thriving race of Hermaphrodites.

Maphs were fine people.

Hook knew as he raced out over the concrete, an invisible presence to the people in ordinary time on the strip, that maphs were very fine people indeed. Very special people; and Shaeel the most special of them all. He guessed that Karg had been dying to know if Hook had ever been up Happy Trail with Shaeel, and he'd damned well let him sweat that one out. That wasn't for the record books!

Mind you, all these sentiments presented Ryder Hook in the most maudlin of maudlin aspects. Hook wasn't a nice person at all. He knew that. It didn't worry him.

He sped about the spacefield doing nasty things to various items of equipment. There was much mischief a man might get up to if he knew what he was about. He left the starpacket *Watchling* severely alone, with the exception that he lifted the guns from the three guards by her airlock and jimmied the aperture and power controls so that they'd blow up when fired. That ought to give Shaeel and Karg – and the kid –a chance.

When he was ready he selected the flier he wanted – a heavier and more powerfully armoured job than the one he'd wrecked in the reception area – and prepared to step aboard. He cocked an eye up at the central traffic tower. If a Boosted Man looked out of the window at the field, he would be able to see Hook speeding about, speed time or not. Nothing had happened, and so Hook knew the Boosted Man up there had not looked out of the window.

He pressed the remote control button on the rig he'd lashed up and, all over the field, fires and explosions crashed out. He even surprised himself with the mayhem he caused. A Boosted

Man had so much *power* – it was frightening and disgusting – the word power acted like a drug on the imagination.

The armoured flier moved across the field towards the air lock. Hook had cracked the security code – it was a standard formula pattern index – but he didn't bother to use it.

He nudged the armoured flier into the line of approach and triggered her Tonota two-fifties. The two guns took out the valves like tissue paper. The backlash of energy washed over the flier and recoiled and through that holocaust Hook swung forward. The same procedure on the outside valves would mean an emergency situation within the dome. He knew doors would slam shut within the buildings, and so Shaeel and Karg and the kid would be safe; but the resultant confusions would keep the personnel here interestingly occupied.

In the crash of the explosions as fuel tanks went up, as tower-pylons cut through and fell, as energy beams fizzed off targets they were never meant to find, as water and electricity got together spectacularly, Hook shot the flier out through the shattered airlock. Air whooshed out after him and someone took a shot at him, which he anticipated and avoided by a superb and arrogant display of aerial effrontery.

The fires whirled towards the shattered exit as the air sucked out. Then emergency shutters rolled across and the bods inside could get on with clearing up the mess.

Hook set course for the city.

If necessary he would use the same method to gain entrance.

As it was, he guessed the Boosted Men would open up the valves to admit him, unlimber guns on him, and seek to take him to find out just what kind of man he was. He hoped they had no idea he was a half Boosted Man. If they didn't and he smashed on through they would have an incredibly harder task clearing up the city.

The Boosted power remained with him for some time and then as the city came in sight it waned. But it did not entirely vanish and then, like the passing away of a trifling spot of vertigo, it returned and he was once more a fully Boosted Man.

A Novaman had set out in a flier to the city to follow him.

Hook gleed.

The black bastards were bringing their own destruction upon themselves! Now he was Boosted he could operate.

He did.

Ryder Hook felt himself to be a man who disliked waste. He abhorred destruction. Senseless baying over an act of vandalism sickened him. He didn't like smashing things up – well, not ordinary things belonging to ordinary people. He'd smash up everything he could belonging to the Novamen. Then, he supposed, being human, he'd take the usual human atavistic and primitive kick from seeing pretty fireworks and hearing big bangs and jump with joy when things fell down. A hundred or so centuries of evolution were not long enough to eradicate all the dark and primordial chasms from the mind of man.

Allied to that would be the typical superficial thinking of the critics who would point to the fact that he became a superman – as they'd phrase it without understanding the agonising gulfs separating him from any sense of superhumanity – only when another superman came near. How convenient, they'd chirrup, how handy to become as superhuman as your enemy when he turned up! Of course, the critics would miss the darker side of it, they usually did. The reality of that situation was far more profound and baffling than a simple equation. The tragedy lay in the fact that Hook ought to have been a Boosted Man and wasn't. He wanted to be. And he knew to what depths of evil that desire might lead him. But temptation could only be resisted by constructing a whole shaky but stabilised life-style around some belief. Hook's beliefs ran deep and dark and, however naïve they might appear to the critics, they powered him and made him a man.

Sod the critics, anyway. He was Ryder Hook, one time assassin Jack Kinch, and he had to save a bunch of near-strangers from a ghastly death and he had to get Shaeel and ves baby and Karg out of it, too. That was quite enough to be going on with for now, thank you.

As he had anticipated the airlock valves to the city waited with the outermost opened ready for him.

Cheeses and traps were familiar gambits in the full galactic life.

Hook barreled the flier in and refused to answer the call from the screen. He slowed as the rear end of the armour slid past the open outer valves and they began to close together. He waited until they were three metres apart and then pushed the speed controls to full forward.

The flier kicked and shot ahead. It smashed its armoured snout into the inner valves. They creaked back on their supports, shuddered, and then gave way in a coruscating crash of metalloy and armour-glass and plastic. Tubing and wiring snaked and curled back. At once flames shot up from severed connections, flames which began to hurl themselves towards the outer airlock valves in the wind-rush. As the valves clunked-to the flames gyrated, swirled, and then fastened greedily upon anything combustible within sight. Hook sent the flier belting forward at full throttle. They'd have those flames under control within seconds, and he wanted to be well away into the city before then.

Only three shots reached him this time, and all three flamed off the armour. He ducked the flier into the first intersection past the landing area out of sight of the heavier weapons.

The flier had warmed up from those three blasts. He checked it over a cross street where a warehouse marked 'Off limits' thrust its bulk up at the dome. Hook thumbed the canopy open, held on to the speed controls just long enough to flick them into drive and then, switching to speed time, dropped clear.

The flier arrowed off across the city and as Hook landed lightly on the warehouse roof he saw the flier punch slap-bang into the side of the warehouse across the street. It blew up. Bits and pieces of plastic sheeting shot into the air. Débris fell. The goons might think he'd been killed in the blast. Once a Boosted Man arrived and took over he would make no such assumptions.

In fast time Hook raced down through the warehouse past frozen robots caught in the act of clearing out empty packing cases, darted into the street, tore along. Stark naked as he was – apart from those old boots – the air-friction that would have crisped mere material felt like a warm breeze on his Boosted skin. The worry nagging at him concerned Anthea.

All the passenger survivors, the only people here he could save because everyone else was as good as dead already, would be coming off shift together around now. But Anthea – she'd been transferred. Lord knew when her shift would come off duty.

Still in speed time he caught a goon around a corner out of sight and yanked the fellow's Tonota Forty free. A light tap and the goon lay on the ground. Hook removed his uniform tunic and pants and put them on as he ran, hopping along on one leg. He had to slow a little; but the lake-side restaurant rose ahead and he could count on finding Rafflans and Myza and Denis and the others there.

He walked into the tumbledown rusty old shed and at once saw the survivors sitting on crates and boxes at the crazy tables. Rafflans stood up. Not a one of them was eating or drinking.

94

Rafflans said: 'You Terran son-of-a-bitch! You did come back.'
The big Krifman laughed. Other people in the restaurant were
eating and drinking and some couples were dancing. 'I told you
that Marden-reef trembler was junk.'

'Where's Anthea?'

'She's still on shift,' said Myza. She looked distressingly
fragile. 'This is terrible! The filth and squalor – and we thought
– let's get out of here!'

'We will, purry, we will,' said Rafflans, patting her shoulder.

'We can't go without Anthea. Rafflans, start 'em towards the
flier park; but go cautiously. If I'm not there in – give me
twenty minutes – grab a flier and break out. Make for the spaceport. Starpacket *Watchling*. Guy called Karg.'

'Check. And you?'

Myza said: 'Denis is off with his Leona.'

Hook adjusted to the switch. If Rafflans saw anything in
Myza that was his hard luck.

'Find him and bring him. Leona is – Leona's dead.'

'I'll find her,' said Rafflans, 'I owe her. She's a good kid.' He
shook his head. 'She told me she really cared for that creep
Denis. He'll come. I'll slug him and drag him if necessary.'

'Don't miss the boat, Rafflans.'

'You great Terran heap of rejects! I haven't forgotten what
I promised you!'

'You'll be doing yourself a terrible mischief, Krifman.'

'That'll be the day.'

Hook and Rafflans walked out of the restaurant. The other
survivors with the de-activated ladybird bugs in their ears
watched them go as though they took salvation with them.

Outside Hook said: 'I'll fetch Anthea. Don't be late, Rafflans.'

'Don't you be late, either, you – ' Rafflans's face broke into a
broad and beaming smile and he went on in a happy-giggly
voice: 'Sure a great meal in there, officer! It's great to be on
Locus!'

Hook turned his back and waited as the flier patrolled past.
Rafflans could be counted on.

He watched as Rafflans made off and then headed for the
Main Building. He switched to speed time. He did not want
the Krifman to be presented with the incredible sight of Hook
abruptly disappearing from view. Outside the Main Building
he saw the usual gaggle of patrol fliers had been heavily re-
enforced and heavy-lift fliers were winging up into the air from
the loading bays at the side. They hung apparently suspended,

barely moving. He went in and raced across the cracked concrete . . . Bio-medical was marked up and he sizzled along corridors with their frozen people and came out into a laboratory which showed all the usual Locus air of decrepitude and disrepair, of neglect and dust which the battered cleaning robots could never clean. Zombies stood in frozen attitudes in stained and ripped lab smocks. They looked exhausted. He looked for Fraulein Anthea Elterich.

He found her painstakingly patching in servo-mechanisms to a powered exo-skeleton. Her slender fingers remained unmoving with an electronic probe delicately positioned in the mechanics of the skeleton. However neglected Locus and its buildings and people might be, work still went on and he felt he would have to revise his estimate that the Boosted Men were pulling out. Those heavy-duty fliers indicated a consignment was being shipped out. But the work continued. These exoskeletons, the primitive origins of the work that had culminated in the Boosted Men, would be used to give extra power to ordinary human bodies. The Boosted Men were back at their old tricks again, building up powerful dupes to do their dirty work for them, as they had done on Sterkness and Janitra.

Anthea looked distressingly beautiful, dishevelled, oil-smudged of face, her hair draggling around her shoulders. The filthy old lab smock showed a large area of orange through a rent in the side. Hook's anger, usually inwardly-directed, could flower in violent animosity against the Novamen as he looked at this girl . . .

In the cover of a spectrographic unit he could come out of speed time and walk towards her. He felt a dizzy sense of vertigo; but that quickly passed, a mere disjointed thump of his heart.

'Alf!' said Anthea, looking up, her lovely face flushed. 'Whatever are you doing here? And – that's a guard's uniform. Have you joined the guards, then? Why, how wonderful!'

Had he joined the police forces of Locus? He must have, for he was wearing a uniform and carried a gun. Anthea looked gorgeous in her gleaming white lab smock, with her hair perfumed and cloudy about her face. The lab looked clean and bright and wonderful to work in. And this evening he was going to give Anthea a wonderful time on the lake and at the ballet!

Chapter Thirteen

He told her.

'That sounds fabulous, Alf! It's Turko and Solaia and we'll have to be there early to get a good seat. But I can't get over you joining the police.'

'I – ' He felt strange, lumpy and nowhere near as fine and fit as he should be down here on wonderful Locus. He had to pass it off, for nothing was going to interrupt the glorious evening he was going to spend with this glorious girl. He had to lie, and that was a most unusual thing for anyone to do in Locus!

'Oh, I felt like a change. How much longer to – '

He was answered by the knocking-off whistle. Anthea straightened up. She put her slipstick into a pocket of that gleaming white lab smock and took it off and they walked together over to the lobby where she hung the smock on its peg alongside all the other equally gleaming white smocks.

'That's a terrific dress, Anthea. It's new!'

'You like it? You just wait until tonight, Alf. I'm wearing what the vending robot described as an elegantly glamorous evening leisure-gown sculptured to show off the delectable me!'

'I'm hungry already.'

Come to think of it, he was famished.

'Caviar and beefsteak and that very extra-special Woheran-cultivated tomato that does you know what. I'm starving.'

'I'll satisfy you, Alf! You know that.'

He took her arm in a companionable grip and pressed and she laughed and so they ran out and into the waning evening sunlight of Locus. By the Great Salvor! It was good to be alive and have a good job and live on a fine planet like this and all the time be socking money into the account! You couldn't better that in any world of the galaxy!

They crossed tracks until they reached the pedway they wanted and were carried along to their hotel. A hot bath and a change of clothes – he pushed the problem of the policeman's uniform away – and then out to have a gorgeous time on the town. A patrol flier cruised past, circled, came back to hover on its antigravs just ahead of them. Anthea waved, as everyone waved to the police. The two men inside – one a mal, the other a tensor – stepped out and came up to Hook and Anthea.

'Hullo!' said Anthea, brightly. 'Friends of yours, Alf?'

'I – suppose so.'

The mal twisted his tubular ear. 'You're Hook.' His hand brought the Tonota Forty out of its holster. The tensor's high thin shoulders twitched as he unlimbered his own gun.

'You'll have to try elsewhere,' said Anthea, laughing. 'This is Alf. He's just joined the police, so perhaps – '

'Alf. Well, if you'll just step into the flier, Alf. And you'd best come too, tayniss.'

'Oh!' cried Anthea. 'But we're going to the ballet – '

'Later on, that'll be all IQ.'

'Well, I've always wanted to see the inside of a police precinct house, Alf. And we'll meet your new colleagues – '

Hook wondered why they wanted him and why, anyway, he was wearing police uniform. He must have got drunk and played a joke. Well, no harm would come of it, not on Locus!

He put a foot on the armoured sill of the flier. He felt a strange trembling in his muscles, a trilling along his nerve-endings. He turned his head and saw Anthea staring up at him with her laughing face all flushed and lovely, the discreet cosmetics enhancing her natural beauty and not hiding it. Her primrose yellow dress with the subtle curves around breasts and waist – she was wearing a filthy ripped orange coverall, and her face although lovely was exhausted and oil-smeared, and these two goons had called him Hook and were pressing guns into his back!

By all the stars in the galaxy!

Fool! Cretin! Idiot!

He had no ladybird in his ear. And the Boosted Man had taken himself off about some business back to the spaceport, probably, and now he had returned – almost too late. Almost. Hook wasn't going to have Anthea roughed up by these goons.

He switched to fast time as he fell into the flier.

To the guards and to Anthea he would appear to have fallen into the body of the machine. They would see him vanish below their line of sight, obscured by the sill, and would follow him.

In speed time Hook went outside the flier. The two goons stood there, their guns pointing inwardly at empty air. Anthea

98

in her pathetic orange coverall stood, one knee flexed, waiting to board. Hook took the ladybirds out of the ears of the goons, whipped tools from his boot, went to work. Then he shoved one of the ladybirds into his own left ear. He couldn't afford to take that kind of insane chance again.

Just how far the resonances between him and a fully Boosted Man operated depended on a variety of parameters he hadn't as yet been afforded the opportunity of investigating. In space – mega kilometers. Down here – a drastic reduction. And he knew that some Boosted Men channelled more power out than others, so that he could be activated at differing distances. Maybe this bastard of a Boosted Man marshalling the resources of Locus to destroy him had a small radius of power output. It seemed like it.

He vaulted back into the flier, knuckled the two goons as he leant out, and then switched back to real time.

Anthea said: ' . . . love to – oh! What's the matter with the poor policemen?'

For both goons had collapsed to the sidewalk.

'Get in Anthea.' She stared at him, wide-eyed, and he yelled: 'Get in, woman, and jump!'

'Alf . . . ?'

He yanked her into the flier and slammed the canopy.

'Put this in your left ear. And then don't say a word. Take it all in and if you have hysterics I'll tan your bottom.'

She thought it was all some kind of joke . . .

He gunned the flier towards the flier park.

Presently he heard a whispery little rustle of a voice at his side.

'Oh – *Hook*!'

'Yes, Anthea. We're getting out of here. The others are waiting and we've five seconds to meet up with them.'

The flier slewed across the flier park. Down there Rafflans looked up through a flier canopy and waved. The Krifman had selected a large armoured job and the surviving passengers had been packed in. Hook opened up a direct channel to Rafflans' flier. It could be monitored, of course; probably it would be, and that could be useful.

'All set?'

'Denis cannot be found. Myza is frantic.'

'If she wants to stay look for him, IQ. We're not.'

Myza's voice, hot and angry:

'You can't leave him! You can't!'

'I can. There is one of him, and a whole lot of us. There's no choice.'

Rafflans must have dragged her away from the mike, for he came on, sounding more excited than angry: 'You'd just take off and leave the guy, Hook?'

'Watch me.'

Deliberately, Hook swung the flier up over the park and headed out.

Rafflans' voice over the speaker said: 'But – '

'Get moving, you Krifman idiot! The goons'll have you pinpointed now. They'll blow you and all to hell and gone.'

Whatever Rafflans was doing down there, if he didn't lift jets soon Hook would leave him cold. No question.

The big armoured flier rose and shot forward. Hook increased velocity. Anthea, looking out the canopy, let out a scream.

Hook's instant and instinctive manoeuvre swept the flier around in a tight curve. The blast sizzled past beneath them. He let the swing carry on and rolled the flier and swooped. Like most of the smaller patrol armoured jobs she carried a pair of Tonota two fifties up front, relatively large and powerful weapons for planetary work. Hook sprayed the blast all across the goons' flier and watched it frizzle. The armouring might protect easily enough from a spray-back reflection or from something below the two hundred mark; against a two-fifty it melted and flowed like toffee in a tureen.

Both fliers streaked for the airlocks.

This was the tricky part. This was the part where sheer blind luck alone could aid him, although he knew that his Boosted senses could keep him out of mischief by his phenomenally quick reflexes, the people in Rafflans' flier had no such protection.

Well – not exactly that, for they had a Boosted Man riding interference for them. Ryder Hook was that Boosted Man. He could feel the neural currents in his body, fully alive, tingling, filled with zest. He could calculate faster than any computer. He could make instant decisions that no computer could even understand. He rolled the flier's nose towards the airlock valves. They'd been hard at work patching and the temporary rolling shutters were in place and presenting a frighteningly solid wall. Hook shot them out.

Fire lanced up at him; but he flung the flier all over the sky within the dome, the radar deflectors chittering as they coped with the incoming beams and baffled them, reflecting them at crazy angles. A really sophisticated computer might be able to take a crack at forecasting where the random beam-reflections were going; no computer of such complexity existed down in Locus.

Riding cover for the big armoured flier beneath him, Hook swept in towards the airlocks. The dome here curved down to meet the hard inhospitable earth of Merfalla. They would have to go through together and quick; otherwise they wouldn't go through at all.

Rafflans knew what he was about. He had a pair of Tonota three-seventies in the larger flier and these made devastating work of the structures and defences clustered about the air-locks. Hook fancied the Boosted Men must be apprehensive of something to have this kind of weaponry available; and if they were armed against the Untergods and not against Ryder Hook he could take an extra chuckle about that . . .

Their defences were aimed outwards, out on to the planetary surface, and these fliers were constructed to go out there and fight. Coming as they were from inside they were like a pair of exceedingly hard and exceedingly painful boots, kicking the Boosted Men up the rear.

The fliers pelted out through a maze of collapsing masonry, plastic sheeting, shivered shards of armour-glass. Flames and smoke gusted low, out from the shattered airlocks, lacing and dissipating over the alien landscape.

The flier jerked and jounced.

'We made it, Hook! It's all – I'm so – '

'You know what I said about hysterics, Anthea.'

'I suppose you do this sort of thing all the time!'

He felt relief. Fraulein Anthea was all IQ.

'Sure,' said Ryder Hook. 'All the time.'

She chattered on as they sped over the alien landscape. Hook had told her the same story he'd told Rafflans, that he'd come across a ladybird plug and de-activated the booby-trap and channelling circuits and so, putting it in his ear, had had his eyes opened to the hypnosis. One could remember what had happened during hypnosis, even if, when in that unhappy state, most vital memories tended to dissipate. So Anthea knew what they'd been up to in their ramshackle apartment block at night times. The alien sun of Tannenbar was about to sink below the horizon rim. Shaeel and Karg would wait one hour. And this was the night they were going to the ballet, and were intending to follow that with enjoyable sexual athletics . . .

The athletics they were engaged in now were involved with dodging gunfire and hitting goons over the head and getting aboard spaceships. It was a funny old galaxy, right enough.

Hook's Boosted power continued. He had already made up his mind that duty to Anthea and the survivors, as to Shaeel, ves kid and Karg, must take precedence over mere vengeance.

He said: 'I'm putting this on autos, Anthea. Can you drive a flier?'

'A sports job – I've never handled an armoured police job like this before.'

'Controls are basically the same. So if you have to, no problem.'

Cutting in the communications equipment he called out for the spaceport traffic control tower. He angled a sidelight on its extending arm so that shadows lay blackly over his face, and highlights altered the plane of his chin and nose.

'Traffic control. If it isn't urgent, stay off the air.'

'It's urgent and address me as sir! Put me a patch through to Communications. And jump to it or I'll have you stripped and kicked into the city.'

There was an awful lot of pure speculation going there; but Hook had a shrewd idea of the way the Novamen ran an operation. Communications came on. He was just as brutally direct, in best Boosted Man style. 'Patch me through to that starpacket on the apron. The one that's special detail. And jump to it, you useless gonil.'

'Yes, sir.'

Now, if the communications or traffic control operatives didn't have the nerve to monitor the call, he would be put through to Shaeel and Karg aboard *Watchling*. It would appear a normal inter-spaceport call, from this simple triangulation; Hook had often found that simple answers offered most.

'Starpacket *Watchling*.'

Hook chilled.

The face on the screen was not that of Shaeel or Karg.

It wasn't even Shaeel's kid, and that might not be such an impossibility.

A hard, creased, professional enforcer's face stared out at Hook. The blue helmet lowered over the brows. The eyes were as flinty as flint itself, the lips as thin as a knapped edge.

Hook reached to cut the connection, and the goon said: 'We

thought you would call, Hook. Your friends tried to do something foolish and – '

Hook couldn't stop himself, the hot query rushed past his stiffening lips.

'Yes?'

'We have them here, Hook, awaiting your arrival. Then we will find out just what all this is about. The master is not amused.'

Hook shouldn't have been surprised.

After all, Locus was a small, insignificant thing, a pest-item, a quickie. It wouldn't take more than one Boosted Man to run the place, now, would it?

He cut the connection.

'What – ' said Anthea.

Hook said: 'It must be feeding time for a baby about now. I hope, for their sakes, they haven't – '

'Your friends have been caught!'

Hook didn't bother to answer.

The Boosted Man would be as frantic as a Boosted Man ever got to being frantic over the identity of these people who were causing so much grief to his Locus project. The goons were shooting to kill, as was their wont. The Novaman would want to take them alive. If, at this vital juncture, the Boosted Man took off, or his power failed through increased distance, Ryder Hook would be in trouble. As it was, he still thought he had the edge. Had he been in a card game with Shaeel, he'd have thought twice. Risks and chances were part of his life-style.

He called up Rafflans.

'The starpacket is out. There was a ship loading there. Looked fast – a Lehrnen job.'

'Check,' said Rafflans, his face hard and craggy on the screen. 'If they were loading she should be ready to space out.'

'If she hasn't already gone.'

'Cheerful Terran clod-hopper.'

'Idiotic Krifman.'

'Your arms and legs are in serious danger – '

'Use your three-seventies on the north airlocks. Get straight in and don't stop. And look out for Anthea. She'll be running towards you.'

'Oh, no!' said Fraulein Elterich, sitting up straight. 'You're going to get your friends. I'm not running off and leaving you – '

'If I say so, you will.'

'You chauvenistic terrestrial – !'

'Terrestrial what, Anthea?'

'Oh!' She found something in her eye and attended to that.

Rafflans said: 'If you don't make it, Hook, I can't say it was an unalloyed pleasure knowing you. But the galaxy won't be the same without you fouling it up all the time.'

'My sentiments exactly.'

They broke the connection.

This time Hook, in the lighter craft, followed the formidable craft Rafflans piloted into the spaceport. He could see bolts of fire striking off Rafflans' armour. The airlocks went down in a gout of flame. If the spaceport personnel attended to the locks, that would help. If they didn't it would mean spacesuits – he'd bet a sizeable wad they didn't have a baby's spacesuit in there, at that . . .

His thought raced ahead at supernal speed.

He ripped off the police uniform and bent over, naked.

Anthea said: 'What? Now, Hook?'

Hook chuckled. 'You just run as fast as you can across to that spaceship there – where Rafflans is headed.'

From the perimeter guards were racing up, bringing weapons.

The instant the nose of the flier emerged past the still-falling remnants of the airlock, Hook switched into speed time.

Around the perimeter the guards froze in positions of the most grotesque originality. The upward-rolling masses of smoke convoluted and twisted like exposed brains, blackened in fire, hung motionless, dense and choking. Men appeared to halt and freeze in mid-motion, although they ran and worked as fast as they possibly could; they were in normal time, real time. Ryder Hook, Boosted Man manqué, operated in speed time.

He raced around the perimeter and he did nasty and un-sportsmanlike things to the various weapons caught frozen in the act of firing at the two fliers. Their beams of energy still poured out in lethal radiation, for even a Boosted Man could not outrun the speed of light; but for all purposes now everything was happening in the merest fraction of a heartbeat, the elapsed time from the moment he leaped from the flier until the moment he returned microscopically small, measurable in chronons.

He bounded up the pedway ramp into the starpacket *Watchling*.

The goon who had spoken to him over the communications net had been as good as his word. Shaeel, ves baby, and Karg, were seated in the main cabin. Everyone in there sat or stood in a stasis of apparent death-in-life. Hook jimmied the enforcers' guns. He took other guns from enforcers he laid low – a nice little way of saying he hit them over the head – and put them in the fists of Karg and Shaeel. He left a clear run from cabin to the ship's airlock.

He knew he had a great deal of time to play with now; but the instant he switched back out of boosted time the minutes would tick along at their sedate minute by minute speed, and the guns would shoot and men and aliens would run, and there would be, as usual, no time at all.

So he had to have everything exactly correct. One gun left unattended could blow the survivors apart as they ran, could flame Shaeel into slaked ashes.

He double checked. If that black bastard of a Boosted Man looked out of traffic control now he would see the spaceport in frantic upheaval as the two fliers battered their way in. But, also, because he was Boosted, he would see the naked form of Hook running about the spacefield in speed time. Hook sweated that one out. No matter how fast his Boosted reflexes and muscles could speed him over the concrete, a blast from the Novaman's gun would crisp him as though he were a simple adolescent yokel from a farm planet instead of a Boosted Man.

He fancied that the cool analysis of a Boosted Man would keep him chained to his screens and control sets, the monitors, the relays and telltales. The Boosted Man would be running this operation on instruments. That is – if he was truly here and not speeding here in a flier from the city. Either way, Hook was taking a chance, and he knew it.

He came across an enforcer with an orange cloak over his orange uniform. His helmet carried a blaze of gold leaf. Hook smiled. Hook usually smiled when a situation gave him not exactly pleasure but a sense of the fitness of things.

He went to work with equipment from his boots and detached the dinky little wrist Delling from under the enforcer's sleeve. He lifted the guy's belt and holster with the Martian Mega unstrapped snugged in it. By holding the plastileather at his back within the vacuum area as he ran, he knew he could carry it without it burning up. The guns, of course, wouldn't burn under those conditions.

About to leave the glass-fronted office where he'd found this important guard – a Tonota one-fifty was in the act of blasting through an aperture and Hook had so fixed it that it would spray back in a most unpleasant fashion – he spotted the wall safe.

A blast from the Mega blew the door off its hinges. The door moved perhaps a centimetre and then hung, askew and unsupported in midair. Hook wrenched it back. The men in the room would react to that when the time came. Inside were no records, no files except a useless report log on security, and only a plastic wallet filled with money-metal. Annoyed at wasting time Hook scooped up the money-metal and looped the gun belt about it, held the bundle into the small of his back as he took off.

One last chore before he switched back into ordinary time and all hell broke loose . . .

He sprang up the pedway into the airlock of the Lehrnan ship. She was sleek, fast, capacious, and good for a multi-parsec ride through the galaxy. He cleansed her of guards and goons – dragging them down to the airlock and throwing them out. They clustered in the air above the pedway, like a frozen collection of mayflies, motionless and spreadeagled in the ungainly postures of falling. Some of them had been burned by their brutal carriage in speed time. He checked the controls. The ship was in full operative condition, had already been pre-flighted, and as far as he could see was all due for lift-off.

He didn't bother to check what might be in the hold compartments.

Now.

Now he had to see if his precautions were enough, if they were satisfactory, if he had done all that he should have done to save these people who depended on him.

Shaeel.

Yes, Shaeel was his only concern.

Karg, too, of course, and Shaeel's baby.

But the rest of them must take their chances.

Anthea Elterich must take her chance along with the rest.

There was no other way of running accounts in Hook's books.

He took a deep breath and went up to the controls of the ship. Her name was *Proton Star* – but he'd change that.

He sat in the pilot's throne and stared at the screen. It showed the stasis on the field, its light speed impulses perfectly capable of rendering a picture to his Boosted senses. The armament was not unlimbered, and a check showed him that he had the choice of the four blister-mounted Krifarm two-eighties. The other stuff, heavier, would take too long to bring into action.

He hammered the preflighting for the four guns, knowing that as soon as he switched back to real time the operation would instantly finalise itself and the guns be ready to fire.

Now?

Now.

Now.

Hook switched back to slow time.

At once the massive chaos on the field exploded into all colour, all sound, all violence.

Flames spat and sizzled, smoke wafted and choked, men yelled, and guns vomited. Rafflans and his people were out of their flier. Hook saw gun after gun along the perimeter blow up, spectacularly gouting orange flame and gusting into shattered and unrecognisable lumps of metal. Rafflans ran last, shepherding them on.

He saw Shaeel appear at the airlock door of *Watchling.*

The guards he had thrown out fell to the concrete. Karg appeared, brandishing two guns. Shaeel carried a bundle.

Hook spoke into the exterior speakers.

'Over here, Shaeel! Follow that idiot Krifman! And jump!'

Shaeel waved ves free arm and ran.

And Anthea?

Hook thought she wouldn't make it.

He ought to have carried her in reduced speed-time; but real time pressed too close.

She ran.

She raced with flashing legs and streaming hair after Rafflans. Hook scanned away from her, panning the field, waiting for that overlooked lethal bolt to come and whiff the girl into her constituent atoms.

He saw only the disintegrating shards of his handiwork.

There was one precaution he could take . . .

He angled two of the big Krifman two-eighties up at the top panoramic windows of the traffic control tower. He triggered a long long burst.

The windows vapourised. Plastic sheeting whiffed into nothingness. He kept on spraying and took the whole top of the tower off.

The dome above it began to buckle inwards.

Rafflans disappeared below the curve of the ship's midriff bulge. Shaeel and ves baby and Karg hared after the Krifman. And here came Anthea, running with wide-open mouth and flashing legs and her hair streaming.

He waited for the tell-tale to come up on the board saying the outer airlock valves were closed.

A man ran out from the traffic control tower main entrance-way.

The dome buckled and sagged in an inverted bowl.

The tell-tale did not light.

The man ran from the tower.

He ran in speed time.

Hook licked his lips.

The man raced towards the ship and Hook knew that to him everything was in stasis; he would reach the airlock valves in the condition in which they were now; they could never close before he could reach them. Hook's thoughts paced the Boosted Man's speed time dash. In speed time he pressed the button.

The Krifarm two eighty aligned on the traffic control door-way erupted.

The Boosted Man – speed time or no speed time – could not dodge.

He crisped.

And then – Hook's powers began that familiar, nauseous, desolating slide towards normalcy.

No!

Normalcy for a Boosted Man was being Boosted. Now Ryder Hook was being deprived of his real status, was being swept back into the herd of ordinary little people; people he loved and hated, people he rescued and killed, people who were like him – and it wasn't fair! It wasn't fair!

Ryder Hook was no longer a Boosted Man.

The tell tale came on. The valve had closed.

At once, Hook sent *Proton Star* up. She speared up through the dome, splintering it past repair, arrowed away out through atmosphere and up into space.

At normal ship's artificial gravity of one eighth of a g no harm would come to the people passing through the airlock.

Soon they'd all try to come crowding into the control section. *Proton Star* was a real starship, and she would take them anywhere they wanted to go in this region of the galaxy. There would be no pursuit. Hook fancied the Novamen would re-open their activities down on Locus, and he just hoped they would never find out that a half of a Boosted Man had done all that to them. Locus was a foulness, anyway, and should be expunged.

Now he could trip the circuits and look into the hold of *Proton Star*.

Hold-mounted cameras faithfully transmitted to the screens on the control deck just what the starship carried.

He might have known – really, he had known all along what lay ranked neatly, one after the other, in the ship's hold.

Boosted Women.

All in cryosleep, all awaiting their resurrection on a planet where the Boosted Men were building up. Well, if Locus was a foulness, what Locus produced was a foulness, also.

If Hook had been asked by what right he claimed the Nova-men to be a foulness, he would have pointed to what they had done in the galaxy. If anyone had asked him by what right he set himself up to be the judge and executioner, he might not have been able to answer that, might have said he had no wish to be either of those two solemn facets of civilised life. But, having said that, and having seriously considered whether or not to punch the enquirer on the nose, Ryder Hook would have known, without question, that however evil he might be himself, he was well aware of greater evil, and that, for his sins, he must do what he could to prevent that evil spreading.

Now he could hear the others ready to enter the control section.

Anthea would be there, and she would have to face this new relationship between them, the relationship Hook tried to maintain between himself and any beautiful young girl in the galaxy. She was not special any more. He felt the sorrow of that; but Ryder Hook's life was one of apartness and alone-ness, never one to be shared by a nice girl like Fraulein Anthea Elterich.

And Rafflans, the big husky Krifman. No doubt he'd want still to carry on with this business of tearing off Hook's arms and legs and wrapping them around his neck. Well, a swift little punch-up might not come amiss, with the rules carefully observed. Rafflans would be a worthy opponent, at that.

And Karg – faithful Karg. The F'lovett meant a great deal to Shaeel, and so he must mean something to Hook.

And Shaeel?

No doubt the Hermaphrodite would say something like: 'My dear feller 'ook! Of course you've brought a supply of nappies and baby-food?'

Come to think of it – he should have, shouldn't he?

Shaeel could be bloody infuriating all the time.

They'd be in any moment. But there was something Hook must finish first. The hold circuits were separated from the passenger and main compartments, as they must be.

Ryder Hook put his hand on the button. Had he the right? Right or not, he thought he was doing the right thing.

He tripped the switch and unlocked the button and pressed it firmly. The air exhausted from the hold. He thought of those beautiful girls, condemned to death because – because they held, sleeping in their bodies, a gift he craved and was denied? He hoped no one could think Ryder Hook so petty as that.

The air exhausted from the hold and cryosleep became death.

Boosted they might be; but Ryder Hook did not believe they could breathe space.

A voice at the door.

'Oh, 'ook, my dear chappie. A Very Nice Performance, all of it, I Must Say. Now, my dear feller, about those nappies . . .'

THE END

NEL BESTSELLERS

Crime

T013 332	CLOUDS OF WITNESS	*Dorothy L. Sayers* 40p
T016 307	THE UNPLEASANTNESS AT THE BELLONA CLUB	
		Dorothy L. Sayers 40p
W003 011	GAUDY NIGHT	*Dorothy L. Sayers* 40p
T010 457	THE NINE TAILORS	*Dorothy L. Sayers* 35p
T012 484	FIVE RED HERRINGS	*Dorothy L. Sayers* 40p
T015 556	MURDER MUST ADVERTISE	*Dorothy L. Sayers* 40p
T014 398	STRIDING FOLLY	*Dorothy L. Sayers* 30p

Fiction

T013 944	CRUSADER'S TOMB	*A. J. Cronin* 60p
T013 936	THE JUDAS TREE	*A. J. Cronin* 50p
T015 386	THE NORTHERN LIGHT	*A. J. Cronin* 50p
T016 544	THE CITADEL	*A. J. Cronin* 75p
T016 919	THE SPANISH GARDENER	*A. J. Cronin* 40p
T014 088	BISHOP IN CHECK	*Adam Hall* 30p
T015 467	PAWN IN JEOPARDY	*Adam Hall* 30p
T015 130	THE MONEY MAKER	*John J. McNamara Jr.* 50p
T014 932	YOU NICE BASTARD	*G. F. Newman* 50p
T009 769	THE HARRAD EXPERIMENT	*Robert H. Rimmer* 40p
T012 522	THURSDAY MY LOVE	*Robert H. Rimmer* 40p
T013 820	THE DREAM MERCHANTS	*Harold Robbins* 75p
T018 105	THE CARPETBAGGERS	*Harold Robbins* 95p
T016 560	WHERE LOVE HAS GONE	*Harold Robbins* 75p
T013 707	THE ADVENTURERS	*Harold Robbins* 80p
T006 743	THE INHERITORS	*Harold Robbins* 60p
T009 467	STILETTO	*Harold Robbins* 30p
T015 289	NEVER LEAVE ME	*Harold Robbins* 40p
T016 579	NEVER LOVE A STRANGER	*Harold Robbins* 75p
T011 798	A STONE FOR DANNY FISHER	*Harold Robbins* 60p
T015 874	79 PARK AVENUE	*Harold Robbins* 60p
T011 461	THE BETSY	*Harold Robbins* 75p
T010 201	RICH MAN, POOR MAN	*Irwin Shaw* 80p
T018 148	THE PLOT	*Irving Wallace* 90p
T009 718	THE THREE SIRENS	*Irving Wallace* 75p
T013 340	SUMMER OF THE RED WOLF	*Morris West* 50p

Historical

T013 731	KNIGHT WITH ARMOUR	*Alfred Duggan* 40p
T013 758	THE LADY FOR RANSOM	*Alfred Duggan* 40p
T015 297	COUNT BOHEMOND	*Alfred Duggan* 50p
T010 279	MASK OF APOLLO	*Mary Renault* 50p
T015 580	THE CHARIOTEER	*Mary Renault* 50p
T010 988	BRIDE OF LIBERTY	*Frank Yerby* 30p
T014 045	TREASURE OF PLEASANT VALLEY	*Frank Yerby* 35p
T015 602	GILLIAN	*Frank Yerby* 50p

Science Fiction

T014 576	THE INTERPRETER	*Brian Aldiss* 30p
T015 017	EQUATOR	*Brian Aldiss* 30p
T014 347	SPACE RANGER	*Isaac Asimov* 30p
T015 491	PIRATES OF THE ASTEROIDS	*Isaac Asimov* 30p
T016 951	THUVIA MAID OF MARS	*Edgar Rice Burroughs* 30p
T016 331	THE CHESSMEN OF MARS	*Edgar Rice Burroughs* 40p

T011 682	ESCAPE ON VENUS	*Edgar Rice Burroughs*	40p
T013 537	WIZARD OF VENUS	*Edgar Rice Burroughs*	30p
T009 696	GLORY ROAD	*Robert Heinlein*	40p
T010 856	THE DAY AFTER TOMORROW	*Robert Heinlein*	30p
T016 900	STRANGER IN A STRANGE LAND	*Robert Heinlein*	75p
T011 844	DUNE	*Frank Herbert*	75p
T012 298	DUNE MESSIAH	*Frank Herbert*	40p
T015 211	THE GREEN BRAIN	*Frank Herbert*	30p

War

T013 367	DEVIL'S GUARD	*Robert Elford*	50p
T013 324	THE GOOD SHEPHERD	*C. S. Forester*	35p
T011 755	TRAWLERS GO TO WAR	*Lund & Ludlam*	40p
T015 505	THE LAST VOYAGE OF GRAF SPEE	*Michael Powell*	30p
T015 661	JACKALS OF THE REICH	*Ronald Seth*	30p
T012 263	FLEET WITHOUT A FRIEND	*John Vader*	30p

Western

T016 994	No. 1 EDGE – THE LONER	*George G. Gilman*	30p
T016 986	No. 2 EDGE – TEN THOUSAND DOLLARS AMERICAN		
		George G. Gilman	30p
T017 613	No. 3 EDGE – APACHE DEATH	*George G. Gilman*	30p
T017 001	No. 4 EDGE – KILLER'S BREED	*George G. Gilman*	30p
T016 536	No. 5 EDGE – BLOOD ON SILVER	*George G. Gilman*	30p
T017 621	No. 6 EDGE – THE BLUE, THE GREY AND THE RED		
		George G. Gilman	30p
T014 479	No. 7 EDGE – CALIFORNIA KILLING	*George G. Gilman*	30p
T015 254	No. 8 EDGE – SEVEN OUT OF HELL	*George G. Gilman*	30p
T015 475	No. 9 EDGE – BLOODY SUMMER	*George G. Gilman*	30p
T015 769	No. 10 EDGE – VENGEANCE IS BLACK	*George G. Gilman*	30p

General

T011 763	SEX MANNERS FOR MEN	*Robert Chartham*	30p
W002 531	SEX MANNERS FOR ADVANCED LOVERS	*Robert Chartham*	25p
W002 835	SEX AND THE OVER FORTIES	*Robert Chartham*	30p
T010 732	THE SENSUOUS COUPLE	*Dr. 'C'*	25p

Mad

S004 708	VIVA MAD!	30p
S004 676	MAD'S DON MARTIN COMES ON STRONG	30p
S004 816	MAD'S DAVE BERG LOOKS AT SICK WORLD	30p
S005 078	MADVERTISING	30p
S004 987	MAD SNAPPY ANSWERS TO STUPID QUESTIONS	30p

NEL P.O. BOX 11, FALMOUTH, TR10 9EN, CORNWALL

Please send cheque or postal order. Allow 10p to cover postage and packing on one book plus 4p for each additional book.

Name ....

Address...

....

Title ....
(SEPTEMBER)